"Kiss me."

It was only a whispered request but Sophie was so attuned to him she couldn't have missed his words if he was a mile away.

"I don't think that's a very good idea."

"I think it's a terrific idea." One hand moved from around her lower back up to her head as he gently encouraged her lips to come closer to his.

"Clay, I—" She opened her mouth but before words could form, he lifted his head and his lips found hers. They were hungry and he didn't hesitate filling her mouth with his tongue. It was everything she remembered and more.

Part of her wanted nothing more than to give him whatever he wanted; the other part, the smart side of her, wanted to run away as fast as she could.

Only one thing was certain: this attraction to her boss was going to eventually cause a rift between them.

* * *

Lone Star Baby Scandal is part of the series
Texas Cattleman's Club: Blackmail—

No secret—or heart—is safe in Royal, Texas...

Dear Reader,

What does a world-champion cowboy do when he can no longer be a champion cowboy? He becomes an entrepreneur worth billions. Clay Everett is a self-made man and risk taker by nature, and he already has his sights set on his next objective: making his buttoned-up secretary, Sophie Prescott, a permanent fixture in his bedroom. The problem is Sophie wants a home and family, and that's not for Clay. He was engaged once and it didn't take his fiancée a quick minute to walk out after his rodeo accident. The single life suits him just fine.

Sophie Prescott is in love with her boss. The scars he attained from his near-fatal accident with a bull give testament to his raw grit and superior courage and make him even sexier than before. Undeniably sexy. But Clay isn't a family man. Even if he knew their one night of passion gave her his child, she would never force him into something he didn't want.

To me there is nothing as sexy as a professional cowboy. It's in their stride, their slow smile, that aura that nothing can beat them—then they prove it by challenging wild broncos and two-thousand-pound Brahma bulls. Team this with a billion or so dollars and, to me, you have the ultimate hero.

I hope you enjoy the story.

Lauren Canan

LAUREN CANAN

LONE STAR BABY SCANDAL

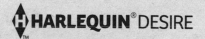

Special thanks and acknowledgment are given to Lauren Canan for her contribution to the Texas Cattleman's Club: Blackmail miniseries.

Recycling programs for this product may not exist in your area

ISBN-13: 978-0-373-83855-4

Lone Star Baby Scandal

Copyright © 2017 by Harlequin Books S.A.

Printed in U.S.A.

www.Harlequin.com

Lauren Canan has always been in love with love. When she began writing, stories of romance and unbridled passion flowed through her fingers onto the page. Today she is a multi-award-winning author, including the prestigious Romance Writers of America Golden Heart® Award. She lives in Texas with her own real-life hero, four dogs and a mouthy parrot named Bird.

She loves to hear from readers. Find her on Facebook or visit her website, laurencanan.com.

Books by Lauren Canan

Harlequin Desire

Terms of a Texas Marriage
Lone Star Baby Bombshell

Masters of Texas

Redeeming the Billionaire SEAL
One Night with the Texan

Texas Cattleman's Club: Blackmail

Lone Star Baby Scandal

Visit her Author Profile page at Harlequin.com, or laurencanan.com, for more titles.

One

When Clay Everett approached, extending his arm in a silent invitation to dance, Sophie Prescott immediately shook her head in embarrassed refusal. Clay was her boss. Her employer. It was a job she valued highly. There should be no mixing business with pleasure even if Clay was the best-looking man at the charity ball. His deep emerald eyes gleamed, framed by dark lashes that matched his ebony hair. His dark tan, five-o'clock shadow and the scar on one side of his face from the rodeo accident that had almost taken his life made his very presence dark and menacing. He didn't need the air of mystery the masquerade ball offered. Since the accident, he presented the persona of a man who was hard and unforgiving, who ate any competition for lunch.

Actually, he had a beautiful smile, perfect white teeth. But he rarely smiled. In his five-thousand-dollar hand-tailored suits and white silk shirts, he gave the impression of the consummate businessman. A man of great wealth who was used to the world of glamour in which he lived.

But when he wore the glove-soft faded jeans, scuffed boots and thin T-shirt that highlighted his six-pack abs and the muscles in his shoulders and arms, it was equally unsettling. That was the Clay she knew. He'd come into their office a couple of times in his Western getup and it was a look she much preferred. Like the raging stallions he trained, like the wild bulls he'd ridden to superstardom in his youth, he was a man unlike anyone else.

Refusing to take no for an answer, he grabbed her hand, pulled her up from her seat and led her toward the center of the Grand Ballroom of the new Bellamy Hotel. Her heart rate tripled. Content to watch the antics of the idle rich from the back of the ballroom, Sophie never expected her boss to find her and propel her into the center of the action. She was a secretary, for crying out loud, a woman who had grown up on a farm in the rust belt of America. She had no business being here, rubbing elbows with the elite of Royal, Texas.

"Breathe," Clay said in his deep, rusty voice, while a glint of amusement sparkled in his green eyes behind the dark mask. "You look as though you're about to pass out. I thought I remembered hearing you say you loved to dance."

"I do. Just not here." And not with him, the president and founder of a billion-dollar corporation and Royal's most eligible bachelor. With those broad shoulders and incredibly handsome tanned features, his presence alone was enough to make everyone sit up and take notice. And not in the midst of people dressed in tuxedos and the latest designer originals, adorned to the hilt with jewels no doubt worth a king's ransom. A few of the other guests smiled at her sincerely, while others smirked in that condescending manner that only someone in her position could recognize and understand. Wasn't Clay being kind to his poor little secretary? How thoughtful of him. Sophie could read their minds without much effort at all.

"And what's wrong with here?"

"If you don't know, I won't waste my breath trying to explain it to you."

He chuckled, a deep, sexy sound that drew more looks from the women within hearing distance. Instead of allowing them to negatively affect her mood, she stopped arguing, closed her eyes and let herself be swept into the music. The band was playing a ballad, one of her favorites. With Clay's arms around her, they danced to the slow rhythm. He smelled so good. A mix of spicy cologne and essence of pure male. The combination was intoxicating. His silken tux jacket felt smooth against her cheek. At some point the song ended and Sophie moved to return to the small table in the back of the great hall.

"No," he said, his warm breath on her ear. And before she could argue, the band struck up another song. He dropped her hand, held her with both arms around her waist, pulled her closer until she could feel every movement, every pulse inside a hard body laden with muscles. More muscles than she'd ever felt on a guy. She didn't know what he did in his spare time, or if such a thing existed for him, but she doubted he sat around knitting sweaters.

One thing was clear: she had his attention and his body hinted at his response. With every slow step, side to side, she felt him move against her belly, driving her crazy. A fog of heat enveloped her as her own body reacted to his. Her hands clutched his broad shoulders and she drifted into a dream world of his making.

Clay was a cowboy through and through. It was in his stride, his way of talking. It was in those deep emerald eyes, so piercing, as though they could see into her very soul. , In those full lips just waiting to cover hers and savor the heat that would surely flare between them. Even the years away from the rodeo arena couldn't weaken that persona. Since the two-ton bull had turned an evening at the rodeo into the nightmare from hell almost ending his life.

The doctors had said he would never walk again, but they didn't know Clay. He had surprised everyone. Everyone except Sophie, who knew Clay was a man who just didn't quit. Ever. After the injuries he'd sustained and the months of grueling physical therapy Clay had been through, it was a pure miracle he was here tonight at all. He'd astounded everyone when he put aside his cane and took to the dance floor, ignoring the limp and the pain that accompanied it.

He'd been America's number-one cowboy, his talent propelling him to superstardom. After he healed enough to be released from the hospital, faced with the fact that he'd never ride rodeo again, he'd found a new outlet for his talents. Today he was a successful cloud-computing entrepreneur, changing his star status from millionaire to billionaire in only five short years. That was just the kind of man he was. If he could imagine it—he could make it materialize. If he wanted it—he got it. And right now, tonight, he wanted her.

Slowly his hands slid down her back, coming to

rest above the surge of her hips, pulling her even closer to him. The feel of his muscled body propelled her to an immediate and impulsive response.

"Let's get out of here," he said in a voice that sounded more like a growl as the third song ended. Without waiting for a reply, he took her hand and led her through the dancing couples toward the exit.

When he summoned the elevator, the doors opened almost immediately with a muffled ding. Stepping inside, Clay pushed a button that sent the elevator skyrocketing to the penthouse where he was staying during the masquerade ball. Then he lost no time gathering her in his arms.

Sophie had been kissed before but never like this. It was raw, passionate—hungry. His tongue traced the line of her lips, moistening them for penetration. He filled her then, his hand clenching her hair in the back, holding her head exactly where he needed her to be. He was so male. His scars that remained from his accident only served to increase his air of desirability.

He had spent his life dueling with the devil and in spite of impossible odds, he had come out on top. Every time except the last. Even then, Clay had pulled his raw courage from someplace deep inside and survived when any other man would have rolled over and admitted defeat. It was part of that rock-hard determination that she felt now, in his arms, his emerald eyes giving off signals as to just what he intended to do to her when they reached the bedroom. He was going to forever change their relationship, and in spite of any thoughts to the contrary, she knew in that moment, she was going to allow it. Blame it on the cocktails, the music or a weakness within her own heart. She had fantasized about this man for far too long. She would probably hate herself in the morning, but tonight she would sample what heaven was like.

At some point the doors opened with an almost silent swish and they stepped out of the elevator into a vestibule with marble floors and occasional tables laden with huge bouquets of freshly cut flowers. Beyond a black door trimmed with gold paint was the penthouse. He guided her inside with a single-minded purpose. It was in his face, in his eyes. He was going to make love to her.

And she was going to let him.

This is wrong, said the small voice in her head. *So very wrong.* He was her boss. Their relationship should be kept strictly platonic. But she followed as they walked toward the bedroom and the word *no* disappeared from her vocabulary.

"Would you care for something to drink?"

She shook her head. If she was really going to do this, she wanted nothing to mar the memory of this night in his arms—a once-in-a-lifetime moment that could never be discussed or thought of again except in her dreams.

He turned a switch and the lights dimmed. He pressed her backward against a wall and his hungry lips again found hers. His shirt and jacket hit the floor before he turned all his attention to her. Leaning over, he kissed her ear, alternately nipping and kissing down her throat until he returned to her mouth, his tongue filling the deep recesses until she couldn't suppress the moan that emerged from deep in her throat. She knew a moment of freedom from the constraints of her strapless gown as it slid down her body to the floor.

Then she was in his arms as he carried her to the master bedroom, his long strides eating up the carpet. When he put her down, the silken sheets of the bed felt cool against her back as Clay disposed of her panties. Then he was hovering above her, directing her lips to his in the darkness. He kissed her jaw, taking little nips as he went toward her ear. It was seduction of the purest form by the master of the game.

"You are so damned sexy," he whispered in her ear, causing chills to run over her skin. "I've wanted you since the first moment you walked through my door."

He continued to kiss his way down her body, nipping at her throat, sucking first one breast then the other, playing with the stiff peaks, teasing until she wanted to scream. Then he suckled her rosy tips, stopping just short of painful, and the feeling burned hot all the way to her core. Then he moved farther down, as though intent on tasting all of her. As he found the spot at the center of her being, he pushed her legs apart and claimed her forever. She opened to him without any rational thought, her mind sent in a whirlwind by what he was doing. She wanted more. But even in her delirium she knew who it was that was about to push her over the edge. Her boss. She couldn't follow the thought far enough to care. Before any further doubts could work their way into her mind, she was exploding, gasping for air, clutching him as the climax went on and on.

One heavy hand remained on her stomach while he opened a drawer next to the bed with the other. She heard the almost silent tear of a packet. Repositioning himself over her he entered her then. Time and all conscious thought disappeared. All she knew was Clay, his scent and the slight rasping of his five-o'clock shadow as he kissed her with full abandon. What was he doing to her body? Incredible things. Touches that singed her until she was drowning in the abyss of his arms. His deep, raspy voice broke the silence as he encouraged her, praised her, whispering raw demands that sent her over the top yet again. Eventually he came with her, his big body straining as they both soared to the heavens. By then she was so inundated with his touches she couldn't rationalize how many times or how long he'd made love to her. Finally, he separated their bodies, placing her head on his broad shoulder, holding her close. She could hear his rapid heartbeat and feel his lungs gasp for air. With a smile, she closed her eyes and nothing existed but the two of them and the gentle, loving space around them.

"Sophie?" Clay's deep voice brought her out of the daydream. "Sophie! Hello? Are you okay?"

A heated blush ran up her neck and over her face as reality came slamming back. She was seated at her desk, staring blindly at her monitor while the phones rang and Clay called her name. She had to get a grip on herself. She kept reliving their one night of passion, first in her dreams then during the day while she was at work. It had to stop. They were attracted to each other but their encounter had taken place more than two months ago and it would not be repeated. It was past time to let it go and move on. Each time he had offered to talk about it, she would find a way to stop him. She didn't want to talk about it. The night had settled inside her heart as a treasured memory. It had happened. It wouldn't happen again. End of subject.

"Yes. Ah…yes. Yep. I'm fine."

"I've been calling your name for five minutes. Are you sure you feel up to working today?"

"Yes. Really, I'm good." She struggled for composure and cleared her throat. If he had any idea of her wayward thoughts, he would never let her live it down. "Just a slight headache. I'll be fine," she lied and reached for the phone.

Clay laid a file folder on her desk with a sticky note attached bearing instructions. Then pursing his lips as though hiding a smile, he walked out the door.

Sophie hadn't realized she'd been holding her breath and released it now in a sigh. It was almost as if he knew what she'd been thinking. Impossible. He couldn't read minds. Could he?

Clay Everett stood in the massive glass-walled lobby of the main barn at the Flying E Ranch. He was surrounded by countless photographs and awards. In the corner were silver-embedded saddles on their holding racks with matching bridles hanging over the horn. Oversize belt buckles with gold and silver inlays were displayed in black velvet-lined shadow boxes. Trophies and large silver cups, the competition date and event imprinted on the front of each, rested on the enormous mantel of the natural-stone fireplace. Still more lined the bookcases around the large room. In between were dozens of action shots of various bulls and horses as they tried with all their might to tear their equally determined rider off their back. If you looked at some close enough, you could hear the angry cries of the animal, recognize the fury in its eyes. But you could also see the grit and determination in the rider's eyes. For the bull, eight seconds to kill. For the cowboy, eight seconds to walk away a champion.

Then there were older pictures of a young boy: riding his first bull, roping his first calf, his legs barely reaching the shortened stirrups of the saddle. The largest picture in the room was of a man holding up a two-by-six-foot check, made payable to Clayton Everett in the sum of one million dollars, proclaiming him the new American Rodeo Champion. Standing next to him were his barn manager, George Cullen, and Sophie Prescott, his secretary and maybe his best friend in the world.

He wandered out of the foyer, down the main hall to the east wing. Climbing up a few bleacher steps that overlooked one of the outside arenas and the sloping fertile pastureland beyond, he sat down, marveling at the view all around him. He would never tire of it. Rolling hills, the few that existed in this area, and white pipe fencing as far as his eyes could see. In the distance a herd of longhorns grazed on the irrigated spring grasses. In the first part of October, hundreds of breeders of Texas longhorn cattle would gather at the Lazy E Arena in Guthrie, Oklahoma, to find out who owned bragging rights to the bull with the longest horns in the world. Word had reached him that his ten-year-old bull, Crackers, had horns three-tenths of an inch longer than his chief competitor's. That should have made Clay happy. But there was more to life than watching horns grow on a damn cow. No one knew it better that he did.

It had been Sophie's idea to move his office from his Dallas headquarters to the ranch. At least temporarily. But the arrangement had turned permanent after almost two years. The maze of awards from his cowboy days had been cleared out and moved to the main barn lobby and the workings of his current office had been moved in. Sophie had overseen the move and, as usual, he couldn't help but be impressed. He'd slid into the burgundy leather chair behind the massive mahogany desk like it was still at the high-rise in Dallas. Everything, from files to computers to office equipment to Sophie's office, had been arranged almost exactly the way it had been at the other location, thereby eliminating the need to learn a new setup. He could find his way around the new office blindfolded.

He'd given Sophie free license to do what she wanted with the trophies and awards that had hung for years in the current office space. She'd done it all while he was still in the hospital, his gut torn open by an angry bull named Iron Heart, his left leg shattered by pounding hooves. In the blink of an eye, Clay had been thrown from the animal and gorged before landing squarely on his head, the compression causing him to break his neck, barely missing his spinal cord. It had taken less than six seconds, from the moment the chute door opened to the crack he heard from within and sweet oblivion, which brought his days as a superstar in the Professional Bull Riding League to an end. He'd known a bull like that would someday come his way. It was inevitable. Nothing went on forever.

She'd had a glass room built in the foyer of the main barn and moved everything there. She'd set about filling it with memories of his life. From boy to man. From child to champion. It was both shocking and humbling. Lord, he'd come a long way over some of the worst roads in the country. He'd also traveled some of the best. The road to Cumberlin County and the Brahma bull who'd awaited him was a culmination of the worst and the best that could happen to a man. The accident had come as close as possible to ending his life but at the same time, it had brought out the true colors of Clay's money-grubbing fiancée, who had suddenly lost interest, finally admitting she simply could not marry a man who had to limp to the dance floor. She'd refused to be saddled with a "cripple" for the rest of her life. She had packed her bags and disappeared faster than a cube of sugar in a cup of boiling coffee. And she hadn't even had the guts to tell him herself. No, the news had been relayed as gently as possible by Sophie.

It had been just one more setback to add to the list. Clay had had to accept that his rodeo days were over and his life was going to change. Hell, it already had. Once he'd been released to come home, it had taken a month of prodding by the stubborn, unshakable, relentless Ms. Sophie to get up off his ass—as she'd put it—and do something. Clay had started tinkering around with some ideas, found one he liked and threw himself into developing it. It was partly to keep his mind off the injuries that were still healing and partly because that was the way he was built; he was a self-made man and risk taker by nature. And Sophie never let him forget it for a second. He loved nothing more than a challenge, regardless of whether it was a two-thousand-pound Brahma bull or a billion-dollar company. A challenge was still a challenge.

He'd set about building a cloud-computing company he named Everest, specializing in providing ironclad infrastructure to corporations. With the usual Everett finesse, it took off like a rocket, making him a multimillionaire almost overnight with no indication it was anywhere near slowing down. And neither was he. No one who really knew him was surprised. He knew only that he wasn't ready for his life to be over. At thirty-four, it was too soon. But while he was forced to set aside the thrill of bull riding, there were other trials to be fought and won.

Like what to do about his attraction to Sophie Prescott.

As if on cue, she popped her head around the corner.

Two

"I thought I would find you here. What do you want for lunch?"

When he merely shook his head, she said, "Then I'll have Rose grill a steak and throw some sides together. It should be ready in about thirty minutes."

"I'm not hungry."

"That's too bad. You've got to eat. Nothing good is going to come out of you sitting around with your head in the clouds."

"I was thinking, not daydreaming."

"Thinking, huh? I'll bet. More than likely thinking about that old bull and how you would do it better if you had a second chance."

He glared. "I'll be in for lunch in a few."

She tapped her watch as a silent way of saying she would expect him sooner rather than later.

Damn, she was beautiful. For reasons he couldn't understand, she chose to tone down her natural beauty, pulling the amber hair into a ponytail and using very little, if any, makeup. Not that she needed any. Her sky-blue eyes couldn't hide behind the glasses always perched on her nose. And those full, slightly pink lips… A man could lose himself in them. And he had done exactly that almost two months ago, the night of the Texas Cattleman's Club masked ball held at the Bellamy Hotel.

It probably shouldn't have happened but that was one thing he would never regret. As his eyes had surveyed the large ballroom and the people seated at the linen-covered tables, Sophie stood out like a diamond set against dark granite. He hadn't been able to resist taking her hand and pulling her out onto the dance floor. Sophie had protested and he understood her side. She felt herself to be only a secretary who had no place dancing with her boss. He didn't give a damn.

She'd driven him crazy for most of the time she'd worked for the company, deflecting his teasing in complete innocence. If she had given him so much as a wink or a beguiling smile, he would have jumped her bones in a heartbeat. But the ever-proper Sophie never did even though he sensed a few times she wanted to. The attraction between them was there. The sparks went off like static around them every time they got close. He'd just never been able to get her to admit it. At the ball, with her in that dress, he hadn't cared. He had to have her. Period.

As much as she was beautiful, she was also about as ornery as a mule. His father had called her persnickety. Let Miss Sophie get her hooks into something and she would not let go no matter what. For the years she'd worked for him, those talons had grabbed hold of his hide and she was damn near vicious in her efforts to guide him in the direction she wanted him to go. She'd been there ever since that day in the hospital, his lowest day, when she'd stood in the doorway, her arms crossed over her chest, and calmly stated with absolute resolve if for one second he thought he was just going to lie in that bed and rot away, he could think again. Giving up was not an option. If he didn't agree with her, he was a jackass. And he was going to have to fight her tooth and nail, day in, day out, before he would be allowed to just give up. It was time for the pity party to end. *They* had work to do.

She'd never strayed from his side. Even on his worst days when his self-pity and self-loathing overcame his common sense, she was there, taking the verbal punches and flinging back a few of her own.

Clay didn't know of another human being who could talk to him the way she did that day. Not and get away with it.

And it continued through the months of therapy. She accepted no excuses, daring him to shut her out, and with each day his respect for her grew. What she ever saw in this broken-down, scarred ex-cowboy he would never know. It wasn't about money. She had never asked for a raise in salary and had, in fact, purchased some office supplies out of her own pocket and never said a word about it. He'd happened to find a receipt. When questioned she'd said only that it wasn't very much so why bother anyone for the money? He had insisted she set up an account at the local office supply store, then had to make her promise to use it.

Most people tended to cower at his anger and between his injuries and the stab in the back of his ex-bitch from hell, he'd had plenty to feel angry about. Rage often filled him but even when he lashed out, Sophie never batted an eye. He owed her his life. That was a fact no one could dispute. And that made her even more tempting than she'd even been before.

He had given considerable thought to the possibility that his attraction to her was because for him, she'd become a nurse, a psychiatrist, a trainer, a cook and sometimes a shoulder to cry on. All wrapped in one beautiful package. But it wasn't because of anything she'd said or done. It wasn't just because she was hands down one of the most beautiful and intelligent women he'd ever met—and yet it was all of those things and more. Clay wanted her. In his house. In his bed. Twenty-four-seven. And he'd tried. But for reasons he didn't understand, Sophie refused. Nor would she let him touch her again. Damned frustrating. If this was some kind of misguided ploy to get him to notice her—to want her— it was working. But when was it going to end?

Instead of returning to the house, she joined him on the bleachers without a word, resting her arms on her knees and fiddling with a wild flower she'd found somewhere.

"So what's on the schedule for today, boss?"

She knew the answer: nothing. But she asked anyway. She always did.

When he didn't answer, she proceeded to give him a few choices. "You've left your cloud-computing business in the hands of others far too long. It's past time you picked up the reins." He sniffed at the pun and watched her grin before she continued. "The cows are calving. You have six new foals on the ground. Jonesy said they all looked top-notch. After lunch, why don't we head to the foaling barn and check them out? I love seeing the new foals." *And you used to*, she didn't say. After two years, he'd learned what Sophie didn't say held as much weight as what she did say.

"Okay." He shrugged, knowing full well she would badger him all day if he didn't agree. He hadn't been down to the foaling barn since the accident. It had been a place where he'd grown up. A place to plan his future, to dream about all the things he wanted to do in his life. But no more. That life, as he knew it, was over.

"I'll go and check on lunch and give you a ring when it's ready. Can you make it down the stairs by yourself?"

The glare he gave her produced the full grin he loved to see on her face.

"Oh, you poor old soul," she teased, hopping down from the bleachers. "I'll have Nathan come and carry you to the house."

"Not unless you want Nathan hurt."

She giggled and turned toward the house. Nathan was the ranch hand she had called when, just after returning home from the extended stay at the hospital, Clay fell and couldn't drag himself back onto his feet. At six-foot-four and two hundred and eighty-five pounds, Nathan was a close match to Clay in physical size and stamina. He had Clay up and on his way in a fast minute. Since then it had become an inside joke between them. If Clay got stubborn and refused to get out of his chair or dismissed a call to dinner, she threatened him with Nathan. She was playing on his ego. He knew exactly what she was doing, but he let her get away with it most of the time. He was not a damned invalid. He might not be able to swing his leg over a saddle—yet—but he could damn well make it up the stairs by himself.

He recognized that Sophie was well-intentioned. He was almost back to 100 percent except for the limp that would take years to overcome, but she knew that implying he was an invalid pushed his buttons. Few things stuck in his craw like that one did. He had come to accept her methods and her teasing without flinging some nasty remark back in her direction, but many times he'd had to bite his tongue to achieve that end. Her nature was that of a mother hen and one of her chicks had fallen out of the nest. Well, peep, peep. He swung his legs over the edge of the stairs and followed her to the main house, cane in hand.

"You received an email from someone named Conrad Drexler," she told Clay as Rose set a beautifully seared steak in front of him. "It sounded important. He wants you to call him at your first opportunity."

"Yeah, I'll call him after lunch."

"Clay, what's going on? You've been closed up in your office for over a week. Is there something I should be doing? Has something happened?"

"Nope. Not a thing. All's good."

He wasn't telling the truth. She'd learned to look for a slight pulsating under his left eye if he was upset, angry or concerned about something. It never failed. And right now the tiny vein was pulsing for all it was worth.

"Well, everything appears to be going as it should. Everest stock is soaring and the people I've spoken with seem genuinely happy with the quality of service they are getting." She smiled at him. "Word has spread and it's growing unbelievably fast. But I guess you know that?" The business's success had propelled him to the rank of billionaire. After putting his days as the world's top cowboy behind him, he'd also started several other companies and all were doing well, although not as well as Everest.

"Yeah," he answered as he began to cut into the perfectly grilled steak. "So far Everest is doing all right."

When a company stopped gaining and growing at a rate Clay thought was acceptable, he did as he had always done in the rodeo arena: he studied. And studied some more. He'd compiled statistics on every working bull in the circuit and its method of removing a rider from its back. Was the bull a spinner, a kicker, did it rotate its shoulders and if yes, in what direction and to what degree? What were its weaknesses and its merits? He took into account age and lineage and any other factor he could find on any one cow and by the time he pulled up to the rodeo arena, he knew every bull in the lineup inside and out. It didn't matter which one he drew, he knew more about it than the owner did. The same went for the industries where he did business.

But knowledge was only a part of the puzzle. Where it ended, Clay's tenacity took over. When he set his mind on something, accomplishment was usually just around the corner. He had a knack for business, was a genius with numbers and statistics, and developing and running a company came as naturally to him as breathing was for everyone else.

But something was going on. If she couldn't figure it out, she would have to wait on Clay to tell her. Oftentimes that wasn't until he had managed to solve the problem. She wasn't usually called in unless things were nearly out of control and he needed her help. She supposed all she could do at this time was watch his body language and be prepared for anything.

"Aren't you going to finish your lunch?" Cole asked as she stood and walked toward the door.

"Not really hungry. See you later."

"You pulled me all the way back to the house with a lecture on eating right—then you don't eat?"

She shrugged. "I'll get something later."

With a sigh of frustration Clay picked up his full

plate, a napkin, cutlery and his drink and disappeared inside of his office, closing the connecting door between their offices. Drexler was one of the men who'd helped Clay develop Everest. What the exact purpose of his call was, Clay hadn't said. He played his cards pretty close to his chest until his idea took root or problem was solved.

If anyone called him an entrepreneur to his face, he would laugh it off and respond by saying he was just an old cowhand who had run into some luck. In truth he was a shrewd and intelligent businessman who seemed to have a natural ability to turn dust into gold.

The bull that changed his life years ago didn't merely crush his leg and open his belly. It figuratively ripped open his heart, challenging his mind and his spirit. As his injuries healed, inside he'd carried frustration, rage, sadness, a touch of hopelessness and always a hint of the bitterness he tried to hold back. Emotions he managed to conceal from most people he couldn't hide from her. Sophie knew that handsome face better than she knew her own. She could tell when he thought someone was lying, when he was holding back his anger, when he thought something was inappropriately funny. She knew when the sparkle that lit his emerald-green eyes meant to come forward or turn tail and run. Most women made the mistake of running the wrong way—straight into his arms. A few weeks later, whatever they'd had—or thought they'd had—was over and no doubt they were still wondering what had happened.

She hoped she would never again see the pain Clay tried to hold inside. Or the fury. But some of it was still there. The hurt, the bitter embarrassment and pure rage that his ex-fiancée had caused. Sophie had to surmise that was the reason he still hadn't dated very much since the accident.

He was the most intelligent man she knew. He had a remarkable sense of humor that was slowly coming back. But it was his deep emerald-green eyes and the rare smiles on a face that still took her breath away even after the five years she'd been an employee. His hands, callused and powerful, could be gentle when he touched a woman, as if he were stroking a newborn foal. The spicy cologne mixed with his natural scent drew females like bees to a flower. Except Clay Everett was certainly no flower. He was hard, raw and pure male.

The accident and subsequent changes he'd had to make in his life shortened his temper and did nothing to improve his attitude. If anything it gave him a dangerous edge, which ironically, to most women, was even more appealing. The same power that held a one-ton bull beneath him was still harnessed inside him; in the bedroom a woman knew it was there. And Sophie knew firsthand just how sexy the man could be after that night of too many cocktails and too many steamy looks at the masked charity event in May.

The next morning, as the sun appeared over the distant hills, she had slipped from the room, dressed and headed for her car. It had taken all weekend to shake herself loose from the spell he'd cast, and even then her life would never be the same. She could feel it. But Monday morning when it was time to report to the Flying E for work, she'd done so with her head held high. She'd brushed past him straight into her office space with a brisk good-morning and refused to look straight into his eyes. That night had been a mistake and it would not be repeated. If he had any ideas to the contrary, the quicker he forgot them the better for all concerned.

It was just too bad no one had given Clay the memo.

Three

Friday morning Sophie opened her eyes and focused on the clock on the nightstand next to her bed. Seven o'clock. She had the day off. The local weatherman had predicted beautiful weather and she knew exactly how she was going to spend the day. After tossing back the covers, she stood from the bed and quickly pulled on a pair of jeans and a T-shirt. Clay was in Dallas attending a meeting with some of his stockholders, so the day was her own. She had a chance to take a beautiful horse and roam over fifty thousand acres of Texas hill country just waiting to be explored. Since moving his office to the ranch and her own relocation to Royal, Texas, she had taken advantage of Clay's generosity in allowing her to borrow one of his many horses and ride to her heart's content.

Foregoing her usual morning coffee and dry toast, she drove the six miles to the Lazy E Ranch. After pulling her car up next to the barn, she entered the main building and headed down the right-hand hallway. The smell of freshly cut alfalfa and sweet-corn molasses swirled around her on a gentle breeze. She heard Hopper nicker before she reached his stall.

Clay had been surprised that first day he'd found her in the main barn. After she explained that she'd been raised with horses and really missed them, he had quickly assured her she was welcome to ride any horse at the ranch during her time off. It became addictive. She'd chosen a black-and-white paint named Hopper. He seemed as eager to leave his stall for an adventure as she was to leave the office. In no time she had checked his hooves, given him a quick brush and thrown a saddle on his back. After that first glorious day, Sophie never missed the chance to go riding.

About the time she led him out of the barn toward the north gate, Clay's voice hailed her. Surprised, she turned toward him.

"Well, good morning," she said, coming to a stop. "Did you cancel your meeting?"

"Yeah. I have to go into Dallas next week anyway so I decided to meet with the stockholders then," he explained. "It's a beautiful day. Mind if I tag along?"

Yes. "Of course not." She tossed the reins over Hopper's neck near the saddle and gave him a friendly pat. "So has the doctor given the okay for you to swing up into a saddle?"

"I haven't really asked for permission."

"And you're doing it anyway." It wasn't so much a question as a statement.

"I think I can still mount pretty good. I don't expect to have any problems."

Ornery man. She refused to take the bait. She'd glanced once at his face. His eyes glistened and a shadow of a smile touched those succulent lips. It was the look of a shared secret he was daring her to tell. Their night together had been incredible but it absolutely would not happen again.

Sophie watched as his long strides carried him toward the bank of stalls that housed some of the top quarter horses in the state. Clay's limp was evident. The horses welcomed him with soft knickers; they watched Clay pass by with large brown eyes, their ears alert. The road to recovery had been long and she had to admire his tenacity, his determination to regain 100 percent dexterity. He had amazed the doctors whose predictions for his future were not so bright. She had firsthand knowledge of just how physically fit the man was, which was why his coming with her made her nervous. In the weeks after their night together, Sophie had used the increasingly busy days in the office as an excuse to prevent any mention of that night they'd shared. If Clay had picked up on what she was doing, he'd said nothing. He had never brought it up and neither had she. But this wasn't the office. She owed it to him not to mention any business concerns and thereby allow him to escape the rat race for a few hours. But it also left her without the barrier to more personal conversation. She had no idea what she would say if he introduced mutual attraction into the conversation.

Today with the cooler temperatures, Hopper was full of spunk and ready for an adventure. Clay returned with his choice of mount, a large chestnut gelding. When both horses were saddled and ready to go, they rode toward the main gate that opened onto the eastern pasture.

It was an area much like where she'd grown up. The first time she'd saddled a horse and ridden out and away from the main homestead, she'd felt the stirring of homesickness for the first time in over a year. During her time off, she sat in the small house she was renting on the edge of town and wondered if she could ever dare to go home again.

Normally, Sophie rode toward the west, following an old cattle trail through the mesquite trees, passing by the mirror-still waters of the natural lakes found in that area. In the direction they were headed this time, the terrain was more rocky, the path steadily uphill.

"I thought I would check a fence as we go," Clay told her. "The ranch hands keep repairing it only to have the wires go down again within a few days. Something's going on that isn't normal. I hope you don't mind?"

"Not at all. I've never ventured into that section of your ranch."

"The terrain is considerably more difficult to cross but once you reach the top, the view is amazing. It's one of the reasons I bought this ranch."

They rode for a while in silence. Then he said, "Tell me how you came to be such a proficient rider. Where did you learn your basic horsemanship?"

"At home," she replied hesitantly. "My dad has a small dairy. We always had a horse or two around. My brother and I grew up riding every chance we got. Mom and Dad both love to ride. I guess I inherited it from them. There are not many things I'd rather be doing."

She saw his lips purse as though he was hiding a grin. "I agree. There's nothing like a good ride."

"I wasn't talking about bull riding."

"Neither was I." Clay leaned down from his mount and opened another gate. He waited while she rode through then closed it behind them. Sophie rolled her eyes and shook her head at his try at an off-color remark.

"How about you?" she asked. "Were you raised with horses, cattle and such?"

It seemed silly to ask the question of a man with his history but while she knew and certainly appreciated his abilities as a cowboy in the arena, she knew little about his childhood. Before moving his office from a downtown high-rise to the ranch, they hadn't really had the opportunity to talk as they did now.

"Yep." A slow grin lit his eyes. "I was put in a saddle when I was still wearing diapers. Being a cowboy was all I ever wanted to do until I hit my teens and discovered the opposite sex."

"You were sure good at it."

"I had my moments." He glanced over at her, the lights in his eyes dancing wickedly. "I was a pretty fair cowboy, too."

Sophie groaned and shook her head. She'd walked right into that one. But the quiet laugh from Clay made it worth it. Since the accident he never laughed, rarely smiled.

"In the years we've worked together, I don't think you've told me anything about your life. Now I know you grew up on a farm. Tell me more."

The question about her past was not expected and Sophie felt tension run rampant.

She hoped he would let the subject drop. Unknowingly he was causing her to remember the horror that had propelled her to run from her home and travel as far away as she could go. Not that those memories ever left, but packed down in the back of her mind they were easier to contend with. No one knew her here. No one had any reason to know her past. And she preferred to keep it that way.

"There's nothing much to tell. Typical small town. Friday-night football games. Blue-plate special every Wednesday at the only café in town. It rotated between stew and chicken-fried steak. Totally boring."

"What brought you to Texas?"

And that was the question.

She shrugged. "No special reason. Just wanted to live someplace new."

Clay opened his mouth to say something else then thought better of it. Sophie let out a silent sigh of relief. She hadn't been prepared for his question. Next time she would be.

The small sandy trail looped through the trees as they made their way to gradually higher terrain. As they rode along, the trees grew taller and the thick stands of oak were overshadowed by tall, majestic pines. At one point Clay stopped and pointed back in the direction they had just come. The view was phenomenal. Amid the distant pine trees, she spotted the core of the ranch; a large clearing marked the house and separate barn areas. In the distance, horses and cattle grazed on the thick oat grasses.

"The stretch of fence is just over here," Clay offered, nodding his head in that direction.

Sophie followed him over another small rise and dismounted when Clay did. Sure enough a couple of the cables in the fence had come loose. One was lying on the ground. Without another word, Clay set out to mend the fence. It struck Sophie as odd watching Clayton Everett do menial labor. But then what else would she have expected from him? First and foremost he was a cowboy. He would always be a cowboy at heart. And a cowboy mended fences. She could only hope he didn't do any further damage to the ligaments and sinews in his body. She bit her lip to keep from saying something to him about it. She had to stop being his mother and let go of the constant worry. Yes, he'd been through hell and back. But he was better.

Looking around her, she spotted the blue of a small body of water in the distance, just below them to the left. "I'm going over to the lake," Sophie told Clay.

"Good. I'll meet you there when I finish here. Stay on this side of it. The shoreline on the far side is very unstable."

"Will do." Sophie mounted her Tobiano gelding and headed back down the trail. Within minutes she reached the clearing that opened up to the water. It was something out of a postcard: shimmering blue waters circled by red rocks with green sage grass filling in the distance between the rocks and the forest. She dismounted, leaving Hopper to graze while she scrambled to sit on a huge boulder overlooking the lake.

Something in the water caught her eye. She looked harder and realized she was watching a small school of fish. They were feeding on something just below in the shade of the boulder. She wished she had a scrap of bread or corn to toss down and see if they would eat it. Maybe if she and Clay ever came back to this spot, she would remember to bring something.

She realized what she'd just been thinking. She'd imagined them coming back together. This was a rare opportunity to go riding with Clay and share the beauty of the ranch. She might return here someday but she very much doubted if Clay would come with her.

There wasn't a single cloud in the sky and a slight breeze blew the hair from her face and teased the leaves on the trees. Suddenly she felt heavy hands on her shoulders. Cole sat down on the large rock, his legs bowing out around her while he moved to hold her close, his hands just beneath her breasts.

"You pick good places to rest," he said.

"I was watching the fish. Can you see them?" She leaned forward, pointing.

"They're feeding off water-dwelling insects and minnows. I should have thought to bring a collapsible fishing rod. We could take home some trout for supper."

"Are they good to eat?"

"Trout?" He sounded surprised. "You've never eaten trout?"

"No."

"Oh, darlin', we must expand your palate. I'm no damn connoisseur, but you gotta try trout cooked in butter and some spices. Maybe with a potato on the side. I like it best when it's cooked over an open campfire."

"Maybe I'll get to try it sometime."

"Maybe you will. Maybe I can cook it for you."

"*You* can cook?"

"Damn straight I can cook. Nothing fancy but I can fill you up and provide good, hot nourishment."

"I would like that."

His body grew taught. "So would I." He moved down to nuzzle the sensitive flesh of her neck. "Will you let me, Sophie?" He spoke softly against her ear, causing the goose bumps to race over her skin. "Will you let me fill you again?"

Somehow their topic of discussion had changed from simply fishing to something much deeper and more raw. Sophie felt the heat in her lower region as it began to build and intensify.

"I want you, Sophie. You know that."

The night they'd shared was completely wrong and should never have happened. While every cell in her body screamed for him, she would not make the same mistake twice. Suddenly Cole lay back on the huge rock and with an easy twist maneuvered her on top of him, face-to-face. Her forearms rested against his broad shoulders and she looked down into those emerald-green eyes. His body was at once hard and pliant, allowing her body to sink into the power of his.

"Kiss me." It was only a whispered request but she was so attuned to him she wouldn't have missed his words if he was a mile away.

"I don't think that's a very good idea."

"I think it's a terrific idea." One hand moved from around her lower back up to her head as he gently encouraged her lips to come closer to his.

"Clay, I—" She opened her mouth but before words could form, he lifted his head and his lips found hers. They were hungry and he didn't hesitate filling the cavern of her mouth with his tongue. It was everything she remembered and more. Without any doubt Clay was the sexiest man she had ever come into contact with. He was temptation run amok with an element of danger on the side.

Her feelings for him had slowly come about in the months after the accident. But rather than pay heed and stay well away from him, she was drawn to him more than ever. The carefree, fun-loving bachelor, the love-'em-and-leave-'em guy, had been gone, replaced by a man of serious intent.

Part of her wanted nothing more than to give him whatever he wanted; the other part, the smart side of her, wanted to run away as fast as she could. He had a ruthlessness she'd always known was there but felt secure knowing he kept it bottled inside. Since the abandonment by his fiancée, he was no longer in control of the anger and merciless drive. It both drew her to him and pushed her away out of self-preservation.

Only one thing was certain: this attraction to her boss was going to eventually cause a rift between them.

She turned her face away, breaking off the kiss she wanted more than air in her lungs. She realized she was now lying on the huge boulder with Clay above her, her head held in his large hand, his erection pressing hard against the apex of her thighs. Of its own accord, before she could summon the strength to stop it, her body pressed against him. Hard. She heard him moan, deep and hungry, and the heat of desire exploded inside her, igniting every vein. He cupped her breasts, first one then the other.

Unbuttoning her shirt, he pushed her bra aside and his lips and tongue teased the stiff peaks.

Voices. Through the sex-filled haze, her brain picked up on the distant sound of voices.

"Clay," she whispered. "Clay, someone's coming this way."

"Let 'em."

"No! Clay, stop. Please." Her own voice was breathy. The last thing she wanted to do at that moment was to push him away. She was in rapture such as she'd known only one other time in her life: with Clay.

Finally he heeded her words and sat up. He drew in several deep breaths of air then turned toward her, his voice deep and full of determination. "I want you, Sophie. I want you so bad it hurts. One time was nowhere near enough. Mark it down as a friendly warning. I will have you again."

Offering his hand, he pulled her to her feet. She quickly repositioned her bra and began to fasten the buttons of her blouse. Clay watched her with a gleam in his darkened eyes.

Before either could say anything more, three of the ranch hands rode their horses around the grove of pine trees and into clear view.

"We came to fix that downed fence," one of the riders said to Clay. "But looks like somebody already beat us to it."

They continued to talk while Sophie edged her way toward her horse. Mounting her ride, she eased into the saddle, content to wait for Clay from there. Eventually, the three cowboys turned their horses around and headed back to the barn, and Clay faced her with a lopsided grin.

"Well, it was nice while it lasted," he said as he mounted his horse.

"What?" she asked, her brows furled in a frown. "Oh," she corrected as she realized exactly what he was referring to: their brief time in each other's arms.

"Ms. Prescott? You certainly know how to make a man feel desirable." With a shake of his head he reined his horse toward the trail leading back to the ranch. Sophie followed, biting her tongue.

Impertinent man.

Four

The days of summer rolled into Texas, raising the temperatures and bringing thunder that rumbled across the sky, hinting at rain that rarely fell. But despite the heat, both the ranch and the small town of Royal were abuzz with activity. Tonight the Texas Cattleman's Club Fourth of July celebration would be held. A large terrace had been built at the back of the clubhouse building. Complete with retractable awnings in case of rain and a soundstage for the twelve-piece orchestra selected to play in time with the fireworks, this year's festivities were expected to be the celebration of all celebrations. Just seeing the huge deck raised Sophie's excitement level.

She had volunteered to oversee selecting and ordering the wines and ingredients for the various cocktails along with stemware, plates and bowls for the pies and ice-cream dessert. She'd done similar tasks before when Clay held a formal dinner consisting of six courses for fifty couples at his ranch house. Even though more people would be in attendance tonight, this was a piece of cake by comparison.

Earlier she'd opened the door to the clubhouse and stepped into a whirlwind of activity. A dozen or so volunteers each had their assigned task lists. Sophie recognized a few of Clay's ranch hands right off the bat. In fact, she'd caught a ride over with George and Alan. They were the strong arms. Aided by a couple more cowboys from the nearby ranches, they would unload the truck moving all the cases of wine, champagne and various setups for cocktails into the storage room.

Checking off each case, she unpacked the sample of plates and glassware. In light of the occasion, she'd selected an assortment of William Avington china in red, white and blue with gold rims and matching inner gold circles on the plates and matching gold rims on the coffee cups, saucers and bowls. But, as Simone Parker had told her, at only a couple of hundred dollars per setting, it wouldn't be a great loss if some were broken. At that thought, Sophie rolled her eyes and smiled. Not exactly like the Independence

Day celebrations back home where her dad would cook hot dogs on a homemade grill in the backyard while her mom made her family-famous potato salad and baked beans, usually served on paper plates. The beverages consisted of beer for the adults and lemonade for the kids. How in the world had she managed to land in such a totally different world?

"Are you almost finished?" a deep voice asked. She didn't have to turn around and look at Clay's tanned face to know it was him.

"Just about. Did you need me for something?"

Sophie glanced at Gayle Brown, one of the volunteers, who stood tongue-tied in front of her, staring over Sophie's shoulder at Clay. He leaned down to Sophie and whispered, "Ask me that when we're alone." Aloud he said, "Can I offer you a ride home?"

She turned and smiled at him. "That would be great. Thank you."

"Okay, Gayle, where were we?"

"The wine is… We…we were at the wine," she stammered, her eyes glued to Clay, who was casually dressed in his T-shirt, a pair of holey jeans and well-worn boots. He could easily wow the pants off any woman in the room. And he didn't have to be a billionaire to do it.

Sophie hoped the woman wouldn't literally start to drool.

"And…what about the wine?"

"The… Oh. It's here. And the new champagne flutes came in last week. They are expecting about five hundred members and guests, give or take, based on past years. If there are more, the kitchen crew will keep the dishwashers going full-time."

"Sophie, I have a total count of the stemware," said another volunteer, smiling intently at Clay. "Where do you want them set up?"

Sophie looked around the vast room. There was no place for all of the stemware in the main ballroom. "Let's set up a table for each type at points around the room. There are six serving stations. I think we need to break down what type of beverage we will be serving, what glasses we need and put out a large tray for the used glasses at each one. I'm betting there will only be enough room for thirty to forty glasses. The rest will have to be brought from the back as needed."

"Okay. Sounds like a good plan to me," Gayle replied. "I'll find Martha and we'll get started on it."

"Perfect." Sophie smiled at Gayle, who had again locked her gaze on Clay. "And make sure each station has plenty of cocktail napkins and stir sticks. Can you think of anything else we missed?"

"Ah. No?" Gayle turned to Sophie. "Some of the guys are manhandling—" she cleared her throat "—the…the ice for the drinks, but like with the glasses, most of it's gonna have to be kept in cold…

ah, hum, excuse me, storage in the back and brought out as needed." She gulped the air deep into her lungs as though she wouldn't have another opportunity. Ever.

"Good enough. Do you happen to know if the two ice sculptures have arrived?"

"No, ma'am. I haven't seen them and I haven't heard anyone talking about them."

"Sounds like I need to make a couple of phone calls. Thanks so much for your help, Gayle."

"Ah…sure. No problem."

"You're not helping." Sophie glared at Clay after Gayle hurried off.

"What did I do?"

She rolled her eyes. "You showed up." She received a pursed-lip smile in response. He knew exactly the effect he had on women.

Clay stood by patiently while she grabbed her cell phone. "Let me call and check on the ice sculptures." She hurriedly placed the call. A few minutes later she was satisfied the sculptures were on their way and all was good. Absently smiling, she turned to Clay.

"All good on the ice sculptures?" he asked.

"Yep. Both sculptures are en route and should arrive in the next hour. Someone else can take over from here."

The day seemed to have gone fast, but by the time she arrived at her little cottage, it would be past six o'clock. Then she could enjoy a long soak in a hot tub and read herself to sleep.

"Members of the club voted to have a pavilion built adjacent to the flower gardens on the west side of the clubhouse," said Clay.

"Yes. I saw it this afternoon. It's nice. I think they will be serving the barbecue there tonight. People can then go inside and be seated at a table or dine at one of the new tables outside."

Excitement ran high. People not associated with the TCC came from miles around to watch what had gained a reputation as the best firework display in the state. Sophie would be happy to watch the fireworks from her little back porch and enjoy a little R & R at home instead.

"Okay. I'm finished. There are plenty of other volunteers to cover anything that might come up."

Most of them only wanted to get a look inside the vast TCC clubhouse. Only a chosen few had ever seen the interior since it was established more than a hundred years ago. Only recently had the club begun to allow select women to become members and while Clay said it was a good thing, many members still didn't like it.

With the warmth of his large hand on her lower back, Clay accompanied Sophie out of the building and to his car.

Once they were both seated in his Porsche Spyder, Clay looked toward her and smiled.

"I'll pick you up at eight. The orchestra will be playing and the fireworks are slated to start at nine."

His words brought up memories of the last time they'd attended a social function.

"I'm not going to the fireworks. I'll just watch them from my house."

"Then I'll watch with you. I have to make an appearance at the club but I don't have to stay long. Would nine o'clock be okay?"

"Clay, I'm tired and all I want is a quiet night starting with a hot soak in the tub. I imagine most of the women that will be here tonight would love your invitation."

"I doubt you're right about that, but at any rate I'm not asking them. I want you to come with me and see the fireworks from the club. I want you to be my guest." His voice lowered. "I want to be with you."

"We are together five, sometimes six days a week," she said and laughed. "Surely you're getting tired of my company by now."

"Never."

"Clay…" It wasn't that she didn't want to be with him. She dreamed of him every night and had recently begun to daydream about him at work, for heaven's sake. It wasn't that she cared about who in the town saw them together or the rumors of a relationship between them that had no doubt spread after the masked ball. After the gossip that had flown hot and heavy in her hometown, a love affair with a billionaire was nothing. But Clay didn't know about those other rumors. And she wasn't ready to tell him. She wasn't ready to discuss that with anybody.

It had been really hard to carry on with her life after the night he made love to her two months ago. Seeing him every day in his office, answering his phone, taking his messages, being polite to the women who called him, making excuses when he wouldn't call them back. He said there was no one else he wanted to talk to unless it was business. About half of the callers didn't want to disclose their business to her. She'd tried and all they said was it was personal. When she filled the top of his desk with message slips, he had glanced over them before tossing them into the trash. At seeing her astonishment, he always responded with a quick wink and that smile that made her heart go ten times faster.

Eventually other rumors replaced the talk about her and Clay and since their relationship really had nowhere to go, she preferred to keep things just as they were.

"Sophie, it's a fireworks display. We'll probably eat hot dogs off paper plates—"

Her eyes flashed to his face to see if he was joking. The mischievous smile he fought to hide told her he was. "Not hardly."

"And watch a beautiful display of lights in the sky while we dance."

He rested his right hand on the stick shift of the elegant Porsche and caught her eyes with his. "I don't want to make you uncomfortable. I don't want to make you the subject of the town's gossips. But I do want to be with you where no phones or computers get in the way."

He pulled the transmission into first gear. "At least think about it. "

She nodded and silently called herself every type of idiot.

In a vehicle that was known to go from zero to sixty in under three seconds, it didn't take long to flash through town and pull up in front of her small cottage. Clay killed the engine and looked longingly at Sophie.

"Okay. Fine. If you're going to make this a big deal, I'll go."

"I'll pick you up at eight." He flashed that sexy smile in her direction.

Sophie nodded. She didn't know if Clay was smiling because he'd won the argument or because he was happy that she was going out with him that evening. In the long run it really didn't matter. She would go. People would talk. She just hoped that the gossip would never reach anyone in her hometown in northern Indiana. Clay was worried about her reputation. He really should be worried about his own.

"Eight o'clock," she confirmed. "Thanks for the ride home."

He waited until she reached the front porch, then was out of sight before she closed the door. Cowboys did like their toys.

The new black stretch limo slowed as it came to a stop in front of the small blue-and-white cottage. Cole had invited Sophie to be his date for the Independence Day celebration and found himself holding his breath until she accepted. He knew several of the men who had called for her over the course of the week and he was pretty sure she'd not accepted any invitation. While he was not willing to commit to another woman—even Sophie—after his ex-fiancée, neither was he willing to take a chance another man would slip in between Sophie and him. She'd hesitantly accepted. In fact, since he had made love to her two months ago after the charity ball, she'd been as fleeting as a deer during hunting season. And so she should have been. Because he was pursuing her. And he would have her again. It was only a matter of time.

After getting out of the limo, he made his way toward the fence that separated her lawn from the street, opened and closed the gate and steeled himself to keep from running to her door. He had never been as infatuated with any woman as he was Sophie Prescott. She radiated sex from the top of her beautiful auburn hair to her rosy-red toenails and everything in between.

He knocked on the door. When she opened it, his mind took her in and his body responded. Sophie was stunning. Wearing a low-cut above-the-knee dress— consisting of layers of navy blue chiffon with tiny glittering rhinestones—and heels that sparkled, she looked stunning. Her long, deep auburn hair had been pulled back at the sides held by matching silver hairpins and diamond earrings. Real or not, it didn't matter. She was spectacularly beautiful. His easy carriage began to stiffen and every muscle in his body suddenly went on high alert. He could feel the heat in his loins and wondered how in the hell he was going to get through this evening with Sophie beside him. He'd thought he was ready to show her a nice evening with fireworks, accompanying orchestra and dancing beneath the stars, but at the moment he could only picture her in his bed, the sheets tangled, their bodies hot and sweaty. The light perfume she wore blended perfectly with her own natural scent, which didn't help the situation at all.

"You look…beautiful." He stated the obvious, then cleared his throat, which had suddenly choked up.

"Thank you." She grinned. "You don't look half-bad yourself."

Together they walked to the limo. He helped her inside and within seconds they were off. He could feel her eyes on him. It was as though she'd never seen him before. He had become accustomed to women reacting to him in different ways, especially since the accident. He was used to everything from starry-eyed fascination to desire, sometimes amazement and often a degree of fear. He'd always had a no-nonsense manner that worked well for him in the arena and subsequently in business. But this was Sophie. She saw through the bogus facade.

Unlike with most women he encountered, he couldn't imagine what she was thinking. They had worked closely together for five years, were in and out of each other's office for most of that time, eventually in and out of each other's life. When she'd applied for the job, she was fresh out of college and felt the role of an administrative assistant would bring her training into play. He couldn't understand how a degree in education would be put to good use if she became a secretary but he'd finally agreed to hire her on a temporary basis. It soon became apparent that he'd been right: she was more than qualified for the position.

His attraction to Sophie had been evident even then and looking back he didn't understand why he'd ever become engaged to Veronica. She'd been born into money and prided herself on getting whatever she set her mind to. Cole had been fool enough to take the bait. He couldn't believe half of what came out of her mouth but she had had her good points, primarily in the bedroom, and apparently, fool that he was, it had blinded him to see only what she wanted him to see. As his popularity grew along with his bank account, women like her had come out of the woodwork. As a man who'd come from nothing, he'd let his ego get in the way of his common sense.

When that bull almost cost Clay his life, at least he'd had the added benefit of Veronica showing her true colors. And Sophie had become even more important to him. He would be lying if he said it didn't hurt that Veronica dropped him because she didn't want to be married to someone disabled. But he was lucky. Most men who played the part of a fool didn't have a Sophie in their life when the rug was effectively yanked out from under them. After years, he had finally managed to seduce her and that was a night he would not soon forget. But there was so much more to Sophie than a romp in bed.

She was the first woman he wanted to be with because he honestly liked her. She was smart and he appreciated that part of her character. He liked the way she thought, the way she talked. He respected her views and that independent streak that shielded her from just blindly going along anytime a suggestion was made. Physically, emotionally, mentally, he wanted more of her and he would have it.

When they arrived at the club, they got out of the limo and made their way to the front steps. He turned his head and met her gaze. It was twilight with a beautiful sunset that part of the country was famous for and Sophie seemed to glow. She was exquisite. The fireworks be damned. He wanted nothing more than to find a dark, private place where he could hold her in his arms and sink into the fire he knew burned within her.

As if reading his mind, she blushed and turned away.

The food had been laid out on back-to-back tables that ran almost the full length of the huge new boardwalk. It smelled delicious. As they walked by, the waiters were just removing the silver domes from over the platters and ringing the tiny bell indicating dinner was ready. Taking their place in line, they were served their selection of meats, vegetables, salads and dessert. Clay then led her to a small table at the edge of the deck that would have a perfect view of the fireworks later on.

"Are you hungry?" he asked, unfolding his cloth napkin and settling it on his lap.

"Starved. But I think my eyes were bigger than my stomach because I don't know how I'll be able to eat all this. It looks delicious. What did you get? The ribs or the sliced beef?"

"I decided to try a little of both."

The tables on the boardwalk were plentiful but they were already full by the time Clay was half finished with his plate. Sophie had already laid her fork down, indicating she could eat no more.

An announcer broke in telling everyone they were preparing to start the fireworks display, encouraging all who were eating inside to come outside for a better view.

Before he could turn the evening over to the team that would shoot off the fireworks, Shane Delgado, the owner of the Bellamy Hotel, stepped up onto the low platform stage.

"Folks," he said into the microphone. "Before we get started, there is something important I wanted to share with all of you." He turned and grinned at Brandee Lawless, the woman everyone knew had stolen his heart. "Brandee said yes!"

No one in the TCC had to be told who Shane was talking about. Or what. You could see the love shining from both of their eyes from two blocks away. A loud clapping, more like a roar, washed over the crowd, accompanied by whistles and plenty of calls of "Congratulations!" to the couple.

"Thanks. We hope you will join us on our special

day. Gabe Walsh and Chelsea Hunt will be our best man and maid of honor."

Sophie glanced over her left shoulder and saw Chelsea positively beaming, she was so happy for her friend Brandee. Chelsea was CTO of Hunt and Co., a chain of steak restaurants. And to Sophie's right sat Gabe, owner of a security firm, his roots in the FBI. He was grinning ear to ear. It was too bad the two of them were merely friends, Sophie thought. They looked like they would be great together. The way Gabe looked at Chelsea from across the room, he maybe thought so too.

The applause erupted all over again. But before Shane could hand the mic back to the announcer, Toby McKittrick, drop-dead gorgeous millionaire rancher, grabbed it. "Since this is a night for announcements, for those who may not know, my wife Naomi and I are having a girl." The broad grin reflected his pride in the woman who had become his life. He'd stolen her away from a thriving career as a as a stylist with her own local cable TV show, though it was rumored she might go back to work after the baby was born. Applause once again broke out along with oohs and aws and calls of congratulations. Their eyes met across the room and it caused a zinging sensation in Sophie's heart.

No sooner had he finished his announcement than the first explosion brought everyone's attention to the sky overhead. The fireworks came in every color in every design you could imagine as the orchestra played music in perfect rhythm with the display.

Clay stole a glance at Sophie's face. With her chin resting on her palms, she seemed totally captivated by what was happening up above. He took his time to really look at her. She was positively drop-dead gorgeous. Her features were near perfection, so delicate. Her lips were full and sensuous. Her neck long and slender. In almost slow motion she blinked, smiled and turned to him. He watched as the light blush covered her ivory skin, the smile faded but the sparkle in her bright blue eyes told him all he needed to know.

His body was running hot, his erection straining against his jeans. He pushed back the chair and stood up He took her hand and pulled her to her feet.

"Do you want to dance?" he asked.

"Really, no."

"The fireworks are about to end. How about if we get out of here before the other cars make it impossible?"

She nodded her agreement.

Still holding her hand, he headed to the front of the building. His limo was immediately brought around. Clay helped Sophie inside then sat beside her. He said nothing. He couldn't make small talk. He'd been in her presence far too long without taking her in his arms. Once he did, it wasn't dancing he would be doing. He needed to be inside her. Until that happened he couldn't retain a rational thought.

"We're going to my house," he told the driver.

"Why?" Sophie asked in a surprised tone.

He glanced at her. "You know why." The long car propelled them forward like a streak in the night. It took fully five minutes to reach the destination, which was four and a half minutes too long. When they reached the ranch house, Clay exited the limo, came around and opened Sophie's door and held his hand out for her. Interior lights had been left on in the house, which made it look even larger than it was during the day. No employee greeted them at the door.

"Where is your staff?"

"Everyone is off for the night."

Clay turned to Sophie. Waiting another minute was too long. He pulled her to him, his lips coming down over hers. She immediately opened to him, accepting the deep kiss and inciting him further with her tongue. His hands found her zipper and rolled it down her back. He began to push the spaghetti straps from her shoulders then realized they were still in the public eye. Knowing Sophie would call a stop, he scooped her into his arms and all but raced up the stairs and into his master suite.

He set her down and made away with the dress. He slid the jacket from his shoulders then began to take off his western shirt, unfastening button by button while remaining focused on her; on what they were about to do. Next went his boots, then his jeans. Standing before him in a beam of soft moonlight, Sophie was exquisite. His hands cupped her face and his lips returned to hers. She was his. And he was not going to let her go for a very long time.

The adrenaline rush slammed his system in much the same way it did seconds before the gate was swung open letting a bull he was riding out of the chute. Cole lifted Sophie and laid her on the bed, his mouth never leaving hers. Her arms came around his neck and he heard her moan as she pushed her lower body against him. Then it was his turn to moan, which came out more of a growl.

"Are you ready for me?" he asked in between nips and kisses to her neck. "I don't think I can hold back any longer. You make me insane, Sophie Prescott."

She opened her legs to him and Clay didn't hesitate. Reaching down, he pushed two fingers inside her, feeling the wet heat that almost seared his hand. With a moan she tilted her lower body upward, impaling herself on his fingers. She was damn close to cresting. He touched her most sensitive spot with his thumb and she went off like one of the fireworks at the July Fourth celebration. He worked her, making it last as long as possible. Then he gently removed his hand and positioned her to take him.

She was breathing hard and he knew she was

beyond communication. He grabbed the small foil packet from his wallet and quickly put the condom on. With his hands he pushed her legs farther apart then cupped her hips in preparation for entry. He felt the tip of his erection meet the core of her body, the wet heat so hot it almost burned, and without any further delay, he pushed inside.

Five

Sophie moaned and there was an instant of hesitation when she pushed against his shoulders. "Cole..."

"You can do this, Sophie. Try and relax, hon."

She wanted to take him. She wanted Clay, period. She wanted to feel him filling her, stretching her tender muscles. She raised her head and kissed and licked the sweat from his chest and neck. A distant drifting memory that she'd sworn she would not do this a second time flitted across her mind. Then it was gone as the intensity of their mating began to grow yet again.

The scents of Clay, his cologne and sex swirled around her, furthering her desire, building yet again to a fevered peak. Clay lost all control, pumping inside her in a raw, animalistic manner. She responded, raising her legs, cupping his head and kissing his sweaty brow. At some point she lost her small grip on reality. The room spun and the sky exploded as together they found completion.

Clay dropped his heavy body to the side, one arm and one leg still covering her. She turned, facing away from him, and curled into his body. With one heavy arm he pulled her closer. She felt him rain kisses over the back of her head. Then she slept.

Her internal clock said it was past midnight when she woke up. Clay was still beside her, his hands playing with the strands of her hair. She smiled and turned onto her back, her hand stroking the beard stubble on his face.

He caught it in his hand and placed kisses in her palm. "Are you all right, Sophie?"

"Mmm, I'm good." She could hear the drowsiness in her own voice. "But it's late. I should go home."

"There's no transportation leaving the ranch tonight. I'm afraid you'll just have to stay right where you are."

"Can I borrow a car?"

He was still for a moment. "What if I said no? What if you were trapped here?" He rolled onto his side and propped his head on one hand, looking down at her. "If I beg would you stay?"

She reached out and cupped his strong jaw, feeling the evening shadow rough against her skin. Her thumb moved over the full lips that could do such amazing things.

"Clay, we've talked about this. You know it's not something I feel comfortable with."

"I want you in my life, dammit."

"You have me in your life. Five and six days a week, eight to ten hours a day. Longer when needed."

"That's not the same thing and you know it." He was silent as though in deep contemplation. "You are hard enough to resist during the day in the office. To know you could be living under my roof, to know I would get to see you and be with you every night as well… I think it would be the best for both of us. That's as lightly put as I can say it."

"I understand." And she did. She was so in love with him that other men just didn't exist. She respected Clay and was flattered by his desire to keep her solely with him. Maybe she was a bit old-fashioned, but why start a serious relationship if you knew from the beginning it had nowhere to go? Clay didn't want a wedding ring and all the trappings that went along with it. She did. He still had most of his life to live and be free. Sophie was the exact opposite. She longed for a husband, a home and kids scampering and playing around the house. She wanted a man with a golden band around his fourth finger that proclaimed he was happily married and proud to let any and all know it.

"If you don't want to move in here then let me set you up in the penthouse of one of my buildings nearby. You would want for nothing, Sophie. You would be close to the horses anytime you wanted to ride." He nuzzled her ear. "And you'd be closer to me."

"I like my little house. It's only four miles away."

"That's four miles too far. If you won't agree to that, either, then let me move in with you."

She couldn't stop the giggle that rose in her throat. "Oh, yeah, I can see how that would work out well. Park your Porsche out on the street."

"I could always drive the truck."

"Let your feet hang over the end of the couch when you sleep."

"Not if I was sleeping with you, which I absolutely would be."

"You would bump your head every time you came into the house."

"Sophie, you drive a man crazy. I know because I'm there."

"I like to make you crazy," she said, rubbing her fingers over the thin line of hair below his belly button.

He took her hand and pushed it lower, wrapping her fingers around his shaft. "Stroke it," he whispered.

She didn't hesitate. The feel of his smooth, silky

skin was in such direct conflict with the rest of his body. Clay rose above her and found her mouth in the darkness.

"What am I going to do with you?"

The words *Anything you want* flittered across her mind. She was so in love with Clay. She could no longer deny it. Even to herself. But he must never know. Clay lived on the fast track and even the idea of tying him down was ludicrous.

His lips came down on hers and there was no more talking for a long time.

Sophie woke before dawn, eased out of bed and hurried to the shower. She couldn't face Clay. Nor could she count the number of times they had made love. Standing under the warming spray, she leaned her forehead against the stone wall and indulged in reliving the memories from last night. He'd positioned her in so many ways, brought her to climax so many times she didn't know if she would ever recover. But that was a great thing. Her body felt well used but more alive than ever.

Exiting the shower, she pulled on one of Clay's T-shirts, gathered her dress and heels, and eased down the stairs in the hopes of finding someone who would take her home. Within minutes she was on her way. She refused to worry about the staff gossiping about her and their boss. Women sneaking out of his house in the early hours of the morning were probably a common occurrence. Or they had been at one time.

The following Monday at work was easier than Sophie imagined it would be. Clay did kiss her good-morning but then sealed himself inside his office, door closed for most of the day. She heard his voice get loud and angry a couple of times and it made her curious to know what was up. The next time he emerged, she intended to ask. This was so out of the norm.

At four o'clock the inner door opened.

"Sophie, why don't you head home. There is no reason for you to stay any longer. I suspect I'll be on the phone the rest of the day." And the door was again closed.

This was repeated the next few days and still Clay didn't reveal what was wrong. The men and women who called sounded upset but didn't care to speak with her. Just Clay. So as soon as his line cleared, she would send the next call through without knowing what was going on.

Days after the siege had started, the high intensity of the calls stopped. Clay began spending more and more time out of his office but that dark side of his personality remained in place.

Trembling, Sophie stood from the bathroom floor. She turned on the sink faucet, then splashed cool water on her face and tried to still the shaking. This was the third time in a week she had awakened to a feeling of nausea. Initially believing she'd picked up a bug, she'd shrugged it off as summer flu and had begun religiously taking vitamin C. But now she wasn't so sure she'd diagnosed her symptoms correctly.

Please no. There was really only one other thing it could be. If she took into consideration the recent intense cravings for hot-fudge sundaes and strawberries with tuna fish, it limited her choice of mystery illnesses down to one. She could be pregnant.

She'd been so seduced out of her mind by Clay the night of the masked charity ball in May, she honestly couldn't swear they'd used protection. Stupidly she hadn't thought about it. Until now. They had made love into the wee hours of the morning. Neither seemingly could get enough of the other. And how many times had he kissed her awake only to take her again? And again. And she'd not wanted him to stop.

She could go on worrying about her suspicion or she could face the facts in a doctor's office. She would make an appointment today. She couldn't think any further ahead than that. After wiping her face, she brushed her teeth and reentered her bedroom to get dressed for work. It had been a challenge not to fall into Clay's arms every time he walked into her private office knowing she must keep up appearances in front of the rest of the house staff. She'd always left her door open for employees to come to her if Clay was otherwise tied up in meetings or on the phone. It would look odd if she suddenly started closing her door. She was probably overthinking the situation, but her mind had ceased to rely on common sense.

But if she was carrying his child, her situation would go from difficult to practically impossible in a heartbeat. If for no other reason than knowing Clay had made it clear a long time ago he didn't need nor want any emotional attachments. Marriage and becoming a father were about as emotional as you could get. With his lifestyle, a child just wouldn't mix. But he had every right to know. This was not something she would keep from him. But that said, she would wait and hopefully choose the right time to tell him.

Right now he was involved with something bad going on with Everest. He hadn't shared what it was but each time one of the board members for that company called, his whole demeanor changed. He never asked her to take a message or tell them he would call them back. Sometimes Cole would open the inner door with fires of anger blazing in his eyes. Other times he would just step through and disappear out of the house. Sometimes the glow on the phone line would go out and still he didn't open the connecting door. Something was definitely up but until he chose to confide in her, all she could do was maintain as much normality as she could.

Sophie stepped outside into the morning light and locked the side door of the little rental cottage behind her. For heaven's sake, she was getting ahead of herself. She was worrying about the outcome of a situation that hadn't as yet been confirmed. Maybe she'd been hit with a flu bug.

And maybe cows could fly.

Clay had just poured a second cup of coffee when Sophie pulled her car into her parking spot. He watched as she opened the door and stepped out. She looked flushed and her brows were drawn into a frown. Not typical for Sophie, who was the most positive person he knew; she always had a smile for everyone. He hoped she wasn't sick.

He couldn't help but speculate what was wrong. Had she received bad news from her family back in Indiana? Was she covering up the fact that she wanted to stop their affair? Technically were they even having an affair? When she was in his arms, she gave him just the opposite impression. He still wanted her to move in with him. Or he wanted to set her up in a luxury apartment closer to the ranch than the cottage she was renting. To hell with what anyone would think. Let the town's gossips do their worst. It was none of anyone's business but their own. He could give her anything she wanted and he wanted to do so. The only thing holding him back was Sophie. A more independent woman he'd never met.

The door opened and the smile of greeting was back on her face. Was he imagining she was working to keep it there?

"Good morning," he said as she put her small briefcase on top of the desk and began taking out her laptop and assorted notes.

"Good morning to you." She smiled her response. "Sorry I'm running a bit late. I seem to have caught a bug. You know, the kind that hits your stomach."

Ah. "If you need to take the day off…"

"No. Thank you, but I'll be fine. If it doesn't let up I might take you up on your offer later on."

Before Clay could walk over to her, the phones began to ring and Sophie, always efficient, began to answer the calls while still unpacking her laptop.

"John Dunn for you on line two," she said then quickly answered another line.

Cole nodded and walked to his office, located directly beyond Sophie's smaller one. For this call he closed the connecting door. Word had reached him a month ago that someone was spreading gossip about his Everest cloud-computing company, even going to the extent of running stories and commenting in online forums about how the mainline computers had been hacked and the information stored there was no longer safe. That Everest had been compromised. He'd had administrative IDs checked out thoroughly to confirm security and systemically reset to new passwords. Sweeps of each area of the system had been painstakingly tested for any virus or malware susceptibility. Absolutely nothing was found.

All security measures were in place and an in-depth security audit had been performed, researching each account on the infrastructure. When nothing came to light, all employees and administrators hired within the past year were scrutinized, their references rechecked, and finally a new interview had been conducted with each, this time by both the cleared administration and the security division. Everything checked out. He couldn't have asked for a better over-all picture of Everest and its working components. If the buyers' information that was stored on Everest had been compromised, damned if he knew how they'd done it.

He had instructed John Dunn, head of Everest security, to run individual reports for each company and have a specialized team review each one. It was thousands and thousands of clients and it would take many man-hours to accomplish. But it was all he knew left to try. Unfortunately, none of it had stopped some clients from pulling their accounts and taking their info elsewhere, which was slowly mounting to millions of dollars lost.

"Yeah, John," he answered the phone, dropping down into his dark brown leather chair.

"Just thought I should touch base with you. We've cleared the larger accounts and are half through the rest. So far we've found nothing to indicate our cloud was breached. The bad news—we had eight more companies pull out last night. One was Stratfire Inc., which, as you know, was a multimillion-dollar account."

"Any luck on finding out who is behind this?"

"We tracked the online articles back to the screen name Maverick."

Clay immediately sat forward in his chair. He knew that name. He'd heard it before. It was some hateful, malicious character who had been blackmailing and exposing the secrets of Royal Texas Cattleman's Club members for months now.

"John, check out that name in relation to the TCC. I'm not the first business he's attacked. We need to find this bastard and shut him down once and for all. And place a call to Sheriff Nathan Battle. He's the sheriff here in Royal. If anyone else has experienced similar, he would know. He should be able to fill you in on what has transpired with the other victims of this Maverick."

"I'll get right on it. Do you have any leads I could start with?"

"Check with Chelsea Hunt. Someone mentioned

she was experiencing similar harassment regarding her chain of steak houses. . I think she may be able to head you in the right direction."

"I'm on it. I'll report back as soon as I know anything."

Clay ended the conversation. Damn. This was crazy. He didn't know where to go next. Probably contacting most of the larger accounts would be a good idea. Offense was always the best defense. Explain to them what was going on and give his personal assurances that everything was fine. It was thousands of accounts. It was time to call Sophie in to help. She was so efficient she could keep the office running in her spare time but in this situation it was probably a better idea to bring in a couple of secretaries to cover the phones and the administrative part of her job while the two of them got busy.

Clay walked to the connecting door and opened it only to find Sophie's desk area empty. A hastily scribbled note on top of her desk said she'd gone home. Cole frowned. He'd call her later to make sure she was okay. Or better, stop by her house and check on her in person. Sophie was not one to miss work. Knowing she'd left concerned him. Once he'd returned to his office, he picked up the phone and called Fran Dodson in his human-resources office. She would have two secretaries there to help him within the hour.

* * *

"Ms. Prescott? The doctor will see you now. If you will please come this way." The nurse smiled as Sophie entered the examining room. Dressed in old-school aqua scrubs, the nurse looked efficient right down to the smile no doubt intended to put the patients at ease. "If you will step on the scale, we can get your weight." Sophie followed the instructions.

Dr. Hutchinson didn't keep her waiting very long at all, which was a surprise. He rushed in through the door, closing it behind him, and held his hand out to Sophie. After asking Sophie a multitude of questions, it came down to the one and only query: Could she be pregnant?

"Yes."

"What symptoms have you noticed?"

"Nausea in the mornings, headache and cravings for strawberries and tuna fish."

The doctor laughed. "That would pretty well convince me. I'm gonna step out for a minute. If you would please change into the gown on the table? We will run a couple of tests while I examine you and we should be able to confirm yea or nay by this afternoon."

An hour later Sophie exited the new multistory medical building in a state of shock mixed with absolute bliss. She was pregnant. She was going to have a baby. She was going to have Clay's baby.

The carefully manicured lawn around the building was bright green, thick and rich. It was a beautiful background for the multitude of flowers growing in the beds nearby. The trees were in full leaf and the birds that made their home there were singing for all they were worth. But Sophie didn't hear them. She didn't notice the flowers or the pleasing scent of the recently mowed lawn. She was two months along, which meant she'd gotten pregnant in May, the night of the masked ball. Their baby would be born in February of the following year.

What would Clay do when he found out? What was she going to do? The best for all concerned would be for her to return to her home in Indiana. She knew her mom and dad would support her through this and she needed that support. They would love her no matter what. They had already proven that.

She didn't want to go back to Indiana. This was her home now. But she knew she couldn't stay here. At least not for very much longer. She had two, maybe three months until she began to show. By then she had to tell Clay. It would be so easy to quit her job and disappear. But she couldn't do that.

Clay had a right to know.

Six

The headline on the front page of the business section of today's *Dallas Times* was Everest Compromised—Millions at Stake. The article went on to say that despite attempts by the founder and CEO, Clayton Everett, business tycoon and former cowboy Hall of Famer, to refute rumors that the company had been hacked, new evidence had surfaced that would strengthen the original reports that Everest had, in fact, been compromised.

Clay wadded the paper and threw it across the room, unable to read any more. The first wave of internet stories that he'd managed to survive would be nothing compared to this. The phones would be ringing off the wall and clients would challenge the security of Everest, resulting in a tsunami crashing to the shore, spreading unparalleled destruction to his life. Without another thought he walked to the inner door.

"Sophie," Clay said as she hung up the phone.

"That was Judge Mathers." She smiled. "He would like a return call ASAP."

"I'll call him. Do you have a few minutes?"

"Sure."

Clay moved aside, indicating she should enter his office. "Please, take a seat. I need to talk with you about something."

She frowned and immediately sat down in one of the two chairs facing his massive desk.

"Have you heard about the rumors that Everest security was breached?"

"No. Clay...? What are you saying?"

"I'm saying someone is trying to bring down Everest."

"Why?"

"That is the question. Along with who is doing it." He loosened his tie and unbuttoned the top button of his shirt. "Actually, it hasn't been breached. The company is solid. Someone is spreading rumors trying to sabotage Everest." He was short and to the point. "This person—or people—is contacting business news sources claiming major security breaches have been found at Everest. As a result, the rumors have spread and our clients have begun pulling their data, leaving multimillion-dollar deals in tatters. Whoever it is has started a firestorm. We've traced it back to several websites and comment forums online. From there it was picked up by the newspaper and it's only a matter of time before it's picked up by TV news."

"Why is someone doing this?"

"That's what we need to find out. The security division has rescreened every employee hired in the last two years. I want to know everything that might sound the least bit suspicious. I want to know who they shared a box of crayons with in first grade. Everything." He looked at her, his expression tired. "You are the only one I trust, Sophie."

She'd gone absolutely ashen.

"Are you all right?" he asked, tilting his head in concern. "You look as though you're about to pass out. Sophie, if you need to go home…"

"No. Ah… I'll be fine."

Clay rose from his chair and shoved his hands inside his trouser pockets. "At this point I'm leaving nothing and no one out. Our clients are starting to withdraw and close their accounts. In the last ten days we're down over thirty percent. The security division is trying to trace back where the rumors started so we have a clear indicator of how far they've come and where they're going with this. Beginning in the morning, you and I are going to hit the phones and contact each and every CEO, president, vice president, owner or founder doing business with Everest and assure them not only are the rumors not true, we are doing everything possible to stay on top of this. We're going to ask for their trust, Sophie. Expect anything and everything.

"Some will tell you right up front they can't afford to take the risk. Others will tell you they'll always stand behind us, then close their account when they get off the phone. Others will say they believe you and that they trust us and prove they mean what they say by picking up the phone and calling as many businesses and individuals as they can to spread the word that Everest is sound. Whoever is behind this is attempting to take Everest down. I've got to reinforce the wall before everything is destroyed."

For several more minutes Clay went over the details to bring Sophie up to speed.

"We will solve this, Clay. I promise," she assured him. "I don't know the whos or the whys of it, but we will find out and save your company."

"I hope you're right."

Clay walked across the room and stared out the large picture window even though he didn't really see a damn thing. His patience had all but run out with the situation. He was livid but he knew he had to hold it together until a solution was found. He walked to the chair opposite, where she sat in front of the desk. Sitting down, he leaned toward her, his forearms resting on his knees.

"I need to ask a large favor. I need to know if you will stay over, here at the ranch, and help me through this. I have meetings scheduled, calls to return, letters to address—the list is long. It would help me a lot if, for a few weeks, you were here and wouldn't mind being called on outside normal business hours."

He could see her hesitation. Staying in his house night and day put a greater temptation between them. At least it did on his side.

"I promise this is all about business," he said as if reading her mind. He held up three fingers. "Scout's honor."

"Were you really a Boy Scout?"

He let out a sigh. "No. But I always wanted to be. Does that count?" He leaned down toward her and cupped her face in his hands. "It will be damn hard, Sophie. But I promise I will do my absolute best to keep this strictly on a business level."

With that he covered her lips with his and bestowed a light kiss. Standing, he took in a deep breath.

"Good way to start." She cracked a nervous grin.

He gave her a crooked smile.

"But I'll do it," she said. "This is a priority. How does one stop a rumor? I don't mean to sound negative but it seems like an uphill battle." She was quiet for a moment in deep contemplation. "Why would anyone spread vicious gossip like this?"

"If I knew the answer to that…" He shrugged. "But what I do know is we've got to get a handle on this and fast. Two secretaries will be here this afternoon. I would like you to move into my office temporarily and help me man the phones. We need to contact as many of the accounts as possible and give assurances that these reports are not valid. I have staff standing by in New York to contact the smaller accounts. You and I will tackle the ones for a million dollars and up."

"You might also call a meeting and invite all the other local business owners or CEOs. They all know you. This was your hometown. I've got to think that they will help you if you ask."

Clay nodded. "Great idea. I'll put together a list and ask you to send out invitations."

"I'll email then follow up with a phone call."

"Good. Probably would be best not to have it here. Reserve a large meeting room at the TCC clubhouse. Arrange for refreshments. Let's make it on July eighteenth, ten o'clock in the morning."

"That's in just over a week. I'll get right on it." She stood.

"Thanks, Sophie."

"No problem. At lunch I'll run to my house and pack a few things."

"Let me know when you leave and I'll pick you up. Someone will spot your car if you stay here. We don't need any more rumors." He winked and it got the desired response.

"Thanks."

"No. Thank you."

Within the next hour the phones began ringing fast and furious with calls from all around the globe. By one o'clock the two secretaries Clay had requested appeared at her desk. One was set up at Sophie's desk, the other at a temporary table next to it complete with a computer and phone. Instructions were given and by noon Sophie was headed to her house to pack a bag and make sure her cottage was closed up nice and tight.

Had she really agreed to stay in Clay's house? He had promised this would be strictly business. She had to believe him. At least she believed he would try to keep it that way. Truth be told, she had no room to talk. However strong his attraction was to her, she could double that if not triple it. Theirs had been a close relationship out of necessity since the day she'd accepted the position as his administrative assistant and ever since his accident.

She thought back on how that time had brought them even closer together. Other than his fiancée, who'd rarely shown up at the hospital, Sophie was his only companion. And he'd needed someone to hold his hand and assure him everything was going to be all right. No way could she have left her boss and friend lying in a hospital bed wondering how to deal with the fact he might never walk again. Those months had changed her and her feelings for this man. And more recently what had started out as her admiration for his strength had turned into unwanted and unexpected feelings of love.

Clearly he was attracted to her, too. But she only hoped his romantic interest in her would soon pass and he would go on to other conquests. Her heart would break, of that she had no doubt. Theirs was an affair that had nowhere to go. And once he found out about the baby, she had no idea how he would react. She had to steel herself to be strong. Cole had made it clear he didn't want a family and if he asked her to marry him when he found out about the baby, it would be for the wrong reason and she knew she would have to say no.

While she was at her cottage gathering the necessary clothing and miscellaneous items, her mind twirled around Clay's statement about rechecking every employee who'd been hired in the past couple of years. She'd been with Everett far longer than that, but what if the incidents of her past came to the surface? What would Clay say? What would he do? It had been written off as a childish teenage prank and no official charges had been filed. But the fact was a man had died and she had been partly to blame for that. The community was small and the rumors had abounded: among the neighbors, in the churches, in the schools. There had even been talk about it in the neighboring counties. The name Sophie Prescott had been linked to the man who died.

Finally she had changed schools and as soon as she received her diploma, she'd thrown a dart at the map and packed her bags. And she had never returned. She didn't know if she could ever go back. But with the baby coming, her options were few.

Her mother had insisted that she could come home, that in the intervening years everything had settled down and there was no reason not to return to her childhood home. But Sophie remembered the taunts and the stares and the fingers pointed at her with whispers of *Isn't that Sophie Prescott? Wasn't she one of the four teenagers who set that barn on fire and killed that elderly man?*

She realized just thinking about it made her mouth go dry and the tears well in her eyes. If only some parts of life were do-overs. She would've never gone to that barn, would never have sat next to her friends as they watched in silent horror as the match's flame had blazed out of control. They had never seen the elderly man who had fallen into a drunken stupor in the corner of the ground floor.

She placed the last of her items in the suitcase and closed the lid. She made sure the little cottage was locked up tight. She had just stepped out onto the front porch when Clay pulled up to the curb in a pickup. He helped her with her bag and they were off.

It was a brief ride back to the Flying E Ranch, down the extended driveway and into a parking space at the back of the house. Clay brought in her bag. If he noticed she was unusually quiet during the trip, he said nothing.

His home left the description of "large" in the dirt. Three considerably sized houses could fit inside his mansion with room to spare. She followed him through the maze of hallways, past more than ten bedrooms that filled the third floor, finally opening a door on the right. The room was as large as her entire cottage.

"The bath and closets are through that door." He nodded toward a single door next to the fireplace. "After you get settled then come and find me. I'll be in my office."

Ten minutes later she entered his spacious office, pulled a chair closer to his desk and with pen in one hand, notepad in the other, she was ready to go to work.

By ten o'clock that evening Clay called a halt to the insanely busy day and insisted on walking her to the temporary suite where she would stay.

"I appreciate you, Sophie." He leaned forward and briefly traced her lips with his. "Good night."

"Good night, Clay."

After closing the door behind her, she walked to the bed and opened the small suitcase sitting next to it. What a day. One full of surprises. There would definitely be a better, more appropriate time to advise Clay he was going to be a father after this situation with his company was put to rest. In the meantime, it would allow her a chance to get used to the idea. She looked down and placed her hands over her flat stomach. Being in Clay's home twenty-four hours a day would make it difficult to conceal the morning sickness. But she had to find a way, for Clay's sake. It wouldn't do to have him worried about this when he had so many other things stacked on his plate. Everest was a major global corporation and God only knew who was trying to shut it down and why.

Over the years, Sophie had met a good many secretaries and administrative assistants of local companies here in Royal. Tomorrow she would begin calling them to see if she might gain some insight as to what is going on. Sometimes the assistants knew as much as or more than their bosses.

She grabbed a T-shirt and some clean panties from her bag and headed toward the bathroom. A long soak in a hot tub of water sounded like it would hit the spot. She picked up the jar of bath beads and the bubble bath, deciding to go all the way. It didn't take long for the huge spa-like bathtub to fill with water. Once she'd shed her clothes, she stepped into the hot bath.

She lay back and just soaked for a long time. Finally, deciding she was about to become a prune, she reached for her shampoo. It wasn't next to the tub. Sitting up, she looked around the room. No sign of it. She must have left it inside of her suitcase. Standing, she then exited the tub and ran into the bedroom. No shampoo inside her bag.

Could it have fallen out somehow when Clay brought the bag upstairs? Chewing her bottom lip, she eased open the outer door. Nothing. Pushing the door open a bit more, she spotted the silver cap of the bottle under the palm plant just a few steps down on the other side of the hall. After looking both directions down the long hallway and seeing nothing, she slipped out of the room and rushed over to the plant. Just as her fingers touched a metal object and she realized it was not her shampoo, she heard her bedroom door click closed behind her.

She rushed back to the door. It was locked! She could feel the blood drain from her face. *Crap!* What was she going to do now? She stood naked in the hall with nothing but a few bubbles to cover her and they were fading fast. She again tried to turn the doorknob in both directions. Nothing. She tried shaking the door. It remained firmly closed.

It was then she heard someone exit the elevator

and walk in her direction. Panic set in every cell of her body. She looked around her, but the only shield was the palm plant. There was no time to question the logic of the idea. She bolted over to the plant, pulled it away from the wall and squeezed in behind it. It stood four feet high and was about the same width as her body but there was plenty of space in between the leaves. Maybe whoever it was coming her way wouldn't notice. Or maybe the person would enter a room before they came this far down the hall.

Her luck wasn't that good. She caught sight of long, muscled legs clad in worn jeans striding past her. Clay stopped a few steps past the plant then turned around and stood directly in front of her.

"I assume you have a good explanation," he said in that deep voice.

"Get me a towel," she whispered loudly, anger lacing her words.

After hesitating only a few seconds, he walked toward her room and found the door locked. Uproarious laughter followed. She didn't know whether she should be furious with him for laughing at her situation or smile at the beautiful ring in his voice. She'd known Clay a long time and it was rare for him to smile, let alone laugh. She decided rather quickly, since she was still in the embarrassing situation, anger was her friend.

He dug deep in his pocket and pulled out a set of

keys, quickly finding one, which he inserted into the lock. The door opened.

"I guess I don't need to tell you these doors have a lock. One tiny little button you push and it requires a key to reopen it from the outside."

"Well, I'm glad you remembered to tell me," she snapped. "Now please move away from the door so I can go inside and finish my bath."

"I'm just curious, what in the hell were you doing running up and down the hallway without any clothes on?"

"I wasn't running up and down the hallway! I needed my shampoo."

"Ah, and you thought it would be out here?" It was half question, half statement.

"No. Yes. I looked everywhere else. I thought you dropped it when you brought in the bag."

He pushed the door open, graciously moved away and turned back toward where she still huddled behind the bush. He offered his hands to help her stand.

"Thanks. I can stand on my own. Just make sure the door isn't locked and thanks for your help."

"Sophie, don't be ridiculous. Give me your hand."

She swallowed hard and placed one hand in his. Just as he began to pull her up, she slid her slippery hand out of his grasp.

"I told you I can get there on my own. Now just go away."

The game was once again on. Catching one slender wrist, he hauled her up from behind the plant, hoisted her over his shoulder and carried her to the bedroom. Sophie squealed and kicked her feet for all she was worth. It did no good at all. She was a one-hundred-and-twenty-five-pound woman and he was used to tossing around five-hundred-pound cows.

Clay set her down next to the bed but instead of making a move toward her, he just stood watching her. Her heart was beating hard in her chest, especially when she looked at his face. He was not going to let her simply go through the door and continue as she had been. He was going to grab her. And kiss her. And she wouldn't let her mind go further than that. With her chin up, she fought to reclaim her integrity and marched into the bathroom. Surprisingly Clay let her go. She felt the need to run but refused to give in to the instinct as she headed toward the tub. Quickly she sat down in the still-warm water with the intent of finishing her bath. She still had no shampoo.

A knock against the frame of the bathroom door caught her attention. She looked up to find Clay holding her bottle of shampoo, a wicked gleam in his eyes.

"It had rolled under the bed."

She reached out for it.

His lips pursed as though hiding a grin. Mischievousness danced in his eyes.

"Now the question is, what will you give me for it?"

Sophie wanted to play this game. But it would set a precedent and the rest of her stay here would be based on her answer.

"Come closer and see," she said softly.

Clay's eyebrows came together in a cautious frown but he proceeded to walk toward the tub. His green eyes gleamed in speculation. Sophie raised her arms to him, silently asking him to bend down to her.

As soon as he did, she pulled him to her lips and kissed him. About the time she heard him moan, she raised the washcloth over his head and squeezed. He jumped back, completely caught off guard.

"You little vixen." He laughed and reached for her again. "Turn around and let me shampoo your hair."

"No. I mean I can do it."

"I know you can, Sophie. Humor me on this one."

Before she could comment, Clay had ripped off his shirt, disposed of his jeans and underwear, and joined her in the tub. She barely had time to grasp what had happened before she smelled the delicate scent of her favorite shampoo as he applied it to her wet hair. Gently his large hands began to massage her scalp and move the suds through her long locks. It felt heavenly, if she could only relax enough to enjoy it. Cupping the water in his hands, he rinsed the soap from her hair. Then his hands moved to her shoulders.

"You are so tense," he murmured, then began to

work the tension away. Her neck. Her shoulders. Her back. "Try to relax."

His heavily muscled legs were on either side of her, dwarfing her own. She closed her eyes and concentrated on what his hands were doing. Then she was lying back against him as his magic hands began to massage her breasts.

"I'm not tense there." She suddenly sat up and spun around.

"Yes, you are," he mumbled.

Then he was kissing her, this time going deep, filling her mouth with pleasure. After a few incredible moments, their lips separated and he drew back.

"Make love to me, Sophie," he growled.

"Clay, I…"

His hand held the back of her head, gently pulling her to him. Then his lips were once again covering hers. She had no resistance. Not even when he lifted her and slowly lowered her onto his erection. Her heart slammed in her chest while the heat in her belly began to burn.

He was incredible, lying back in the huge tub, the water lapping at the tips of her breasts as he filled her. She broke the kiss and sat up, wanting to focus on the dynamic heat between her legs. With only a few moves, Sophie rocketed to the stars, her limp body falling against his chest. His strong arms came around her.

Clay stood and helped her to stand. Together they

stepped from the tub. She felt him place a soft towel around her back as he carried her to the bed. He pulled back the covers and followed her down. Without a word he entered her. His lips were hot as he kissed her mouth, jaw and down her neck, alternately nipping and kissing.

As he took a rosy bud into his mouth and began to suckle, the passion again began to build. When she sensed his hold on his desire slip away, Sophie wrapped her legs around his back and held on. Each stroke became harder, each one deeper than the last. The same precarious intensity that had led him to champion wild bulls over and over again began to come out. It was thrilling, a bit frightening, beguiling, seduction at its best. She felt the breath die in her throat seconds before she was again experiencing an amazing release, taking her up to the heavens, where she stayed while Clay found his own release, joining her in euphoria.

Her next clear thought: She couldn't breathe. The second: She didn't care. Clay was lying on top of her, heaving to catch his own breath. He rolled off her but kept her close, one muscled arm going around her. She felt his lips against the side of her face as he gently kissed her. With his scent surrounding her, she closed her eyes. She was an idiot.

An idiot in love.

Seven

"I have to fly to New York," Clay said as he walked out of his office. "Would you call and make sure the apartment is prepared? Oh—and I need you to come with me."

"Me? Why me?" Sophie was flustered.

"I'm meeting with the Everest board. I need you there to help me prepare and take notes." He turned to face her, and didn't try to hide a full grin. "Don't worry. It's legit. Unless you want it to be something different…?"

"Legit works for me. I'll call them right now. But you know how I hate to fly."

She hoped Clay hadn't notice that her hands were

shaking. *It's the flying*, she told herself. She hated to fly. She hadn't been able to get over the irrational fear since working for Clay. Her job required quite a bit of travel and every time her nerves were stretched to the snapping point. Never mind that this time she would be flying to New York. With Clay.

The penthouse was a large multilayered structure with one of the best views of Manhattan one could ever imagine. The three large bedrooms were equally blessed. He'd purchased the building four years ago and had the space converted, turning the loft into a luxury suite on the top floor of the highrise. A helipad on the outside edge of the same floor took away any necessity for ground transportation from the airport.

She'd felt strange sharing the space with Clay the first time they'd gone there. The second trip was much better. Now here they were again, going to the same penthouse, only this time things between them had changed. A flare of heat ran through her body, settling in the apex of her thighs. She knew what his smile was about. She had the same inner grin. It was never a good idea to sleep with the boss. But after the night they'd spent together in May and the times between then and now, she could think of little else.

If there was ever a man who made a woman feel like a woman, it was Clay Everett. He appreciated the females and saw no reason to be coy about it. But neither was he brazen. He walked a perfect line between the two. When she'd first come to work for Clay, he'd come off a lot more reserved, almost shy. After the accident, he'd changed. Anger and resentment at his injuries and at the woman who'd unceremoniously dumped him because of those injuries had made him hard. From then on, he approached a woman like he did a business deal: straight and direct, sighting his target and focusing, not stopping until results were achieved. No slap-happy cowboy; no easygoing persona. She knew those attributes were still inside him but she hadn't as yet figured out a way to bring those more gentle qualities out. Or if she even wanted to.

Clay had made it clear he wanted her back in his bed for as long as she would stay. But Clay had always said he was not the kind of man to settle down with a family. He now lived on the fast track, as though his time to experience life was limited. He had no time left for frivolities, no time to kick back and have a beer with one of his lifelong buddies. He worked because that was what he did; his life demanded it. He slept and ate because he had to. He had sex because he wanted to. But everything was accomplished with the same driving force. If Plan A didn't work, he went on to Plan B. If a company didn't want to get serious and negotiate, he dropped them and found another. If food didn't set well with his palate, he threw it out and ordered something else. If a woman didn't suit his needs, he went on to the next.

She had to admit this new Clay had advantages. He worked hard and played the same, only both were done with determination and without humor. He'd always put 100 percent into a project or business negotiation but when the project was finished, it was done. In the months after the accident, once he could walk again, he had then kicked up his heels and partied the night away, usually with the woman of his choice, the two of them disappearing for the night. It was as though he was testing the waters to see if any woman would still want him. He got his answer pretty quickly.

But work eventually overcame the need to establish himself with the fairer sex and the one-night stands ended. As Everest grew, his time was filled, his mind totally devoted to business. And then came the night of the charity ball. One too many cocktails and she'd danced into the arms of one very sensuous, unbelievably sexy man: a dark force with a power of persuasion few men ever mastered.

As far as she knew, since that night in May, Clay had not gone on to the next woman. And he was allowing her time, showing a patience he rarely showed anyone about anything. It was the only aspect of the old Clay she could see. But how long would it last?

Sophie wanted a family. She wanted a husband

who would put her and their children first. She couldn't see Clay ever taking on such a role. So she had resolved to keep her heart well out of the picture. It was a resolve that lasted almost a week.

And now there was the fact that she was pregnant throwing a wrench into the works.

The plane was waiting for them when the limo drove up. When she'd climbed to the top of the stairs, she was greeted by Clay's flight attendant and welcomed on board the 747. The luxury didn't stop at his house. Like the barns at his ranch and most everything in his life today, size and opulence abounded. That included his planes, and this one, his newest, was certainly no exception. There was seating for twelve people and plenty of room to move around, a small area where food was prepared, a bathroom, a separate area for the security team so they could unwind and enjoy the flight, a master bedroom for overseas flights and Clay's office. She couldn't help but speculate who else was coming along on this trip. He hadn't mentioned anyone.

Clay followed her up the stairs with his security and six board members in tow. As he stepped into the main area, he gave orders to take off.

The plane-to-helicopter flight took almost four hours. Most of the time in the air they spent discussing the meeting, the agenda and especially the number-one concern: the maniac who had been throwing out slanderous lies about the company.

Arriving at the Everest building, they walked together down the corridor that led to the spacious penthouse suite. Sophie took her overnight bag into the bedroom she'd always used while Clay made some phone calls and continued to address the concerns with the men who had flown in with them. The meeting was scheduled for that afternoon at four o'clock with dinner to be served at eight. She had her agenda, notes of additional topics Clay wanted her to bring up and her iPhone to record the discussion. She was ready to go. The plan was to stay over one night then head back to the ranch in the morning. She couldn't help but wonder what the night would bring.

After a light lunch, they headed downstairs to the large meeting room. There were about twenty people in attendance. Some were new faces but most were men and women she'd met before. In just a few minutes, Clay asked everyone to have a seat and the meeting began.

All the attendees appeared to listen to Clay with rapt attention. After the general meeting, he touched briefly on the situation caused by Maverick and voiced assurances that none of the stories circulating about the security breach was true. Everest was solid. The reasons behind the attack were still unknown.

After the day's business was concluded and dinner had been enjoyed, Clay approached her as she gathered her things.

"Sophie, I have been asked to accompany Joseph Rankston and a few others to a lounge down on Lexington. You are welcome to join us."

"Oh, well, thanks. But honestly, I'd just as soon have an early night." So much for an early night with Clay.

"Are you sick?"

"Nope. I just don't want to sit around some club while the bunch of you conspire as to what you're going to do with the bad guy spreading the rumors when you catch him."

Clay hesitated.

"Go. I'll be fine."

"Are you sure?"

"Of course." She tried to keep the disappointment out of her voice. She'd hoped they would have the evening together. So much for great plans. "To tell you the truth, I'm a bit tired. A hot bath and an early night sound good to me."

"Okay, then. You know how to reach me and the chef for anything you want to eat. I'll see you later."

And he returned to the men and woman waiting for him by the outside door, leaving Sophie standing in the center of the emptying conference room. Grabbing her things, she returned to the suite.

Two of the walls in the main room were floor-to-ceiling glass. She watched the lights come on in the city. All the colors. She decided to take a hot bath, something she especially enjoyed in this bathroom where luxury took on a whole new meaning. A thousand jets circulated the water and massaged her skin. The aroma from the bath salts filled the room, adding to the amazing relaxation. When her fingers began to prune, she toweled off, pulled on her sleeping attire and headed to the kitchen. Cookies and milk seemed like the perfect ending to this day. She opened the center door of the refrigerator that covered the expanse of the wall. Sure enough, on the center shelf, there was a fresh carton of milk, the same brand she'd gone on about the last time she was here. In a gourmet baker's box on the counter were five-inch-wide chocolate-chip cookies. When she had contacted the firm who maintained this apartment for Clay, she hadn't mentioned the milk and cookies. That they kept such copious notes was amazing. She'd only answered yes, she would be coming, and voilà! Plopping onto a stool at the bar, she continued to gaze out over downtown Manhattan as she enjoyed the late-night snack.

After a few rounds of flipping channels on the TV, she finally gave up and decided to go to bed. Much later she was awoken by the sound of a woman's laughter and animated talking coming from the main room near the front door. Then all was quiet before she heard a muffled, "Good night, Clay."

He had gone out with another woman.

While she was here waiting for him, he'd been out doing the town with someone else. The tears welled in her eyes. She felt nausea curling its way up to her throat. Clay Everett would never change and what self-deluding reason had made her think he would? Why in the world would she ever think Clay saw her as special? She was a good secretary, a fair nurse-maid when she had to be. And apparently a fill-in when he couldn't find anyone else.

Just then she heard a soft knock and her door opened. Sophie pretended to be asleep. She didn't want to talk to him and she certainly didn't want anything else from him. Clay walked over to the bed and called her name. She kept still and ignored him. She felt the covers being lifted and placed higher on her shoulder. Then there were quiet footsteps as he returned to the door and closed it behind him.

Self-admonishment filled her heart. She was fin-ished with the man, such as there was to finish. In fact, she really needed to start looking for another job. She couldn't deal with the emotions; she didn't seem able to control them. All she wanted now was to get back to the ranch and back to her cottage. She was taking the rest of the week off.

How could he come into her bedroom from the

arms of another? Brother, could she pick 'em. She was such a fool. She could feel the blush of humiliation cover her neck and face. What must he think of her really? What would he think when he found out she carried his child? Then that question only made it worse. Why should she care what he thought of her? The fact that she did was pathetic.

The next morning, she gazed in the mirror and it looked as though she hadn't slept all night. Then she realized through a befuddled brain that she hadn't. And she was mad as hell. Enough so she couldn't look at him and refused to even try.

"I've got coffee going in the kitchen," he said, giving her an odd look.

"No, thanks." She turned down coffee and anything to eat. In fact, the very idea of food made her queasy.

"I missed you at the club last night."

"I'll bet you did." She forced what she hoped was a cheery smile. Let him frown all he wanted. Better yet, let him figure out what was bothering her—if he should decide he cared.

"Do you have a headache?"

"Not yet. Are you ready to go?"

Sophie didn't care whether he'd finished his coffee. He could eat his Danish in the car or throw it down the disposal. She wanted to get out of here, away from him, and get back home to her own place, where she could think.

"I suppose so." He held his Danish in his teeth while he pulled on his jacket. "Is that all you brought?"

She stood by the front door, her overnight bag in her hand, her purse over her shoulder. Rather than answer she just glared.

"Okay. Let's go."

Before she could walk out the door, nausea hit her hard. Dropping her bag and purse, she ran for the nearest bathroom, slamming the door behind her. *Oh, God.* It was the morning sickness rearing its ugly head. Just what she didn't want to happen in front of Clay. When the moment passed, she sat on the floor leaning against a wall. It was the third time she'd been sick. She'd read it was normal and to expect it, but she'd never considered it would hit her while here in New York. What was she going to tell him?

What did it matter?

She was still furious Clay had apparently gone out with another woman last night, and regardless of how many times she got sick, it didn't change the fact or how she felt about it. For heaven's sake. She was pregnant with his child.

She got to her feet and proceeded to grab a toothbrush, toothpaste and some mouthwash. She wished she had some crackers but wasn't about to ask for any.

There was a knock on the door. "Sophie? Are you okay?"

Oh, yeah, she was great. The temptation to tell him the truth was overwhelming but it was a long flight back. She didn't want to be trapped in that plane with him. She had no realistic idea of how he would react and that was not the place to find out.

"I'm fine. Just too much excitement last evening. Being in New York and everything."

"You don't like New York."

"I never said that."

"You don't like big cities, then. Look, can we not do this through the door?"

She dried her mouth and yanked open the door. "No problem. Ready to go?"

Clay gave her a sideways glance that clearly said his suspicion was up. Let him choke on it. She returned to the front door, picked up her laptop and swung her purse strap over her shoulder. Clay grabbed the overnight bag and tried to take the laptop but she refused. She could carry his child. She could damn sure carry her own luggage.

Following Clay to the helipad, she climbed into the chopper and minutes later they headed to the airport.

Once they were on board, the giant aircraft headed west. Sophie kicked off her shoes and sat back into the luscious, deep, rich leather seat. Her eyes felt swollen and puffy. She knew her face looked ashen. All the more reason to stay away from Clay Everett.

None of the people who had flown down with them were on board. She was curious as to why but refused to ask. Grabbing a small blanket from the drawer next to her, she covered herself, determined to sleep during the flight home. The notes from the meeting could be completed in short order, so she could do that when they arrived. Or perhaps she wouldn't do it at all. Let him hire someone else to type up the notes. If he didn't like it, he could fire her and she'd be on her way back to Indiana, where she should be in the first place.

She heard him behind her in the small kitchen area. It sounded like he was mixing drinks. Who would drink before noon? Then she realized with aggravation, it *was* noon. A five-ounce tumbler appeared in front of her face with amber liquid inside.

"Here, take it. You look like you need it."

"No, thank you."

"Sophie, either you take the drink with a couple of aspirins or I'm having this plane turn around and getting you to a doctor in New York. It's light. Just enough to calm you down a bit."

"I'm calm."

Clay leaned over, placing his face directly in front of hers. "Take. The. Glass."

Still glaring, she reached up and took the drink

in her hand. She held the chilled glass next to her forehead but didn't take a sip.

"Do you want some aspirin?"

"No, thank you."

Clay was quiet for a few minutes. While she refused to look at him, she could feel his eyes on her. He shed his jacket, leaving only the white dress shirt, unbuttoned at the neck. He pulled the shirttail out of his jeans and proceeded to roll up the sleeves. She glanced his way in time to see him nod to himself as though he'd determined the problem. Good for him. He took a seat next to her, his right arm going around the seat behind her.

Sophie immediately moved to the next seat down the cabin-length sofa away from him.

"Please leave me alone."

"I haven't even started to bother you...yet." She heard him blow out a sigh. "Sophie, two people came back to the suite with me last night. Scott and Loretta Bennett. Loretta needed some paperwork she'd asked me to bring on the Ludlow case. Her husband came along when she picked it up."

"I really don't care."

"Then why the tears? Your face is as swollen as a marshmallow that's been roasted over a campfire. Unless you got bad news from home... Did you?"

"No."

"Then," he said gently, "why were you crying

last night? And why are you so angry with me this morning?"

"I never said I was angry."

He gave a half laugh. "You didn't have to."

Clay moved down to again sit next to her and pulled her into his arms. She struggled against him but he was too strong.

"Sophie, there was no woman in my room last night. The meeting and later at the club was strictly business. I know you must have heard Loretta when she came upstairs with me. Sophie, look at me."

He was doing it again. It was a contest of wills and she was about to concede defeat. Slowly, she looked over at Clay. He was the most attractive man. A one-day-old shadow of beard stubble on his strong face highlighted the deep grooves on either side of his mouth. His green eyes were lit from within and watched her carefully. There was no laugh, no smirk.

"You are very special to me," he whispered only inches away from her mouth, his deep voice sending a series of chills across her skin. "I would never do that to you. If either of us should decide to see someone else, I hope we would have the common courtesy to tell the other."

"Is that what you did with your other women?"

Silence. "I'm not saying I'm not a bad boy or haven't been in the past. What I'm saying is you are the one person I would never string along while I saw another woman."

And then his lips touched hers, lightly at first, as though testing to see what she would do. Then his mouth came down on hers, tasting, devouring, over and over. His tongue pushed its way inside and Sophie couldn't suppress a moan. She opened to him and the more she gave the more he took. His big hand slid under her shirt and cupped her breast over her bra. It wasn't enough. Not nearly enough. Then the bra fell away and his hand was on her, squeezing her nipple. The shirt came over her head and his lips found the other breast. A flare of pure lava rolled down to her core.

"Damn, Sophie." He picked her up and carried her toward the back of the plane to the bedroom. Laying her on the bed, he quickly stripped them both of their clothing and pressed her down into the soft mattress.

"You make me crazy," he murmured. "I can't stand being away from you. Not having you every day, every night, is frustrating as hell."

With his knee he parted her legs and settled himself onto her. As he rotated his hips, she felt his erection hard against her center. The impossible thought that they were thirty thousand feet above the ground only added to the need running rampant. Her heart gave a thunderous leap as excitement rushed through her, adding to the heat that already flowed through her veins. Her hands trembled as they roamed over his broad chest. Her entire being began to shiver in reaction to the fiercely male focus on his face. He once again lowered his lips to hers. He was hard, demanding. Then his mouth left to blaze a fiery trail over her throat and down to a pink-tipped breast while his hand cupped the other. The line between pain and sheer pleasure was walked perfectly by Clay, who caused flares of growing, intense pleasure from her breast to her core.

Falling to his side, he threw a heavy leg over hers as if preventing her from moving. His free hand drifted downward over the slight curve of her stomach, until his fingers found the curls of her essence. She was unable to move, frozen by the pure male anticipation that was Clay. One finger made a bold insertion and her body shuddered, all her thoughts consumed by what he was doing. By what he was about to do. She was on the edge of total satisfaction and Clay didn't let the opportunity pass to send her to the heavens. Not caring if anyone might hear, she cried out, her climax consuming all rational thought. Her breath left her lungs when she gazed into his emerald-green eyes, now dark with passion, and saw the look of insatiable arousal. There was no stopping him and she didn't want to. She wanted more. She had to have him inside her.

As though he knew and understood, he rolled on

top of her and pushed inside. The tight, glorious heat filled her to the max. She was on fire for him and couldn't offer enough of herself to him and the power of his big body. With a few circular moves and one hard thrust, she cried out again as their hot bodies writhed together in one harmonious blending of white-hot passion.

Sophie couldn't move. As she lay next to Clay, gasping for her next breath, she felt his arms go around her and hold her close, his lips kissing her forehead and temple.

"Did we overcome your fear of flying?" he joked, still gasping for air, his voice deep from the recent emotion.

"Maybe."

"Then we will have to keep trying until you can tell me you love to fly."

"Hmm." She felt rather than saw him smile as he covered her with a soft blanket. The curious hum of the engines and the gentle swaying of the plane lulled her to sleep. She drifted off thinking that maybe flying wasn't so bad after all.

Eight

Where is the damned blackmail note?

It had been two weeks since the online rumors began and Clay had heard nothing from the person or people who'd instigated the vicious rumors against Everest. Not through any email, no snail mail, no phone call. He would be the first one to admit he was losing it. What in the hell did they want? There had to be a ransom for Everest. More threats. More lies. *Something.* And what was Maverick's involvement in all this?

The only part worse than not knowing what the next plan of attack would be was still not knowing the cause of it. Why was someone doing this? What did they hope to gain?

He had managed to hold his temper in front of Sophie, but excusing himself from the office a dozen times a day when he made trips to the barn to mutilate bales of hay in an attempt to work out some of the exasperation had not skipped her notice.

Over those two weeks, Sophie and Clay worked morning till night, manning the phones and talking with clients of Everest located around the world, assuring them the latest publicity was pure fiction, made up by some crazed individual to try to make Everest fail. Everest cybersecurity was solid and uncompromised, as it had been from the beginning.

Their combined efforts began paying off. The number of businesses canceling their accounts had drizzled down to nothing and amazingly new accounts were coming on board. In the last two days Clay had been advised that the sales staff had taken at least a hundred calls from corporate executives wanting more information on Everest. Pamphlets and application forms were promptly sent out.

Still, he didn't know who was behind the vicious rumors or their reasons for spreading them.

A meeting was arranged with local business owners and CEOs to discuss the Maverick situation. Clay left Sophie and the secretaries to man the incoming calls as he headed for the Texas Cattleman's Club.

To his surprise and delight, the meeting room was full. The hushed banter stopped when Clay stepped up to the microphone.

"I want to thank you all for coming and hope you're enjoying the refreshments provided. I know most of you have a very busy schedule, so with your permission I'll get straight to the reason for this meeting. As most of you may know, the reason I asked you here today was because I need your help. Someone, I don't as yet know who, has engaged in a smear campaign, online and in the local and national media, claiming Everest's cloud computing has been compromised. They claimed security was breached and highly classified information was open for viewing. For the record, none of that is true. Not in the least.

"I don't have a clue who's behind this or what their motivations are. As far as I know, the only real enemies I've ever had walked on four feet, had horns and weighed about two thousand pounds. They don't mess around with computers."

A general laugh was heard across the room.

"But the name Maverick has come up in our investigations, and I know how other TCC members are putting up with harassment and blackmail from this mysterious source. I'm here to ask for your help and support and share what we've found out so far."

"This has been going on for months now." Wesley Jackson spoke up. "We have all tried to determine who is behind this. So far all we have is a little speculation.

"Many of us have been hit by blackmail threats, and attempts to ruin our personal reputations and close our businesses down," added Toby McKittrick. Several people nodded in agreement.

"I think I can speak for most of us," said Cecilia Morgan, "when I say we will do what we can to get behind you on this and give you whatever support you need."

"I'll give you the names of the detectives we have working on this and you can have your security contact them." added Gave Walsh. "At least they will be up-to-date with this character's goings-on."

"We all know other CEOs across the globe that might do business with Everest," Shane Delgado spoke up. Let us contact them and assure them Everest is solid, that you're a good and reputable man."

"I would be deeply grateful," Clay responded, his heart warmed by the show of support.

"Heck," said yet another, "we've all gotta stay together on this until we can determine who the culprit is and shut him down. I think it must be someone we all know or have known at some point in the past. Something we said or did must have rubbed him the wrong way and he's out for revenge. Or he's jealous. Or maybe he is just a nut. At any rate, we've got to work to support each other and we welcome you to the fold, Clay."

As Clay glanced around the room, every head was nodding in agreement. These were good men and women, honest business owners who supported each other, as it should be. That was, after all, what being a member of the TCC was all about.

It took another few weeks but finally Clay's business began to come back on track. Remarkably, because of the publicity efforts, outreach to clients and help from TCC members, Everest overall gained more accounts than it had lost. It was thriving.

"Do you have any plans for lunch?" Clay asked Sophie as she was preparing to leave the temporary desk where she had worked for the past few weeks.

"Well, I was going to pack," she said. "The crisis is over and I need to move back into my own house."

"I want you to stay here, with me." Clay crossed the small space and removed her handbag from her hands. "As I'm sure you've noticed, we have plenty of room. Why do you feel the need to leave?"

"Why do you think I need to stay?" Sophie felt as though she'd been tricked. "I agreed to live here while we battled the rumors, but that's over, thank goodness. There's no more reason I need to be here night and day."

"How about doing it for me? Stay because I want you to stay."

"Clay, please. Don't put me in this situation. It isn't fair."

"I thought we had something going between us. Am I wrong, Sophie?"

She would not answer that question. Yes, they had something but just what it was she didn't know. While the sex was amazing, for her there had to be more. She needed commitment to go with the passion and most of all she needed love. There had to be love. Clay didn't love her. She wouldn't go as far as to think he was using her, though, because it was mutual. But she wanted a future, especially now that a little one was about to enter the picture. Clay couldn't give her that.

"Is it right to ask me to stay while you needed my help then try laying a guilt trip on me when I need to go back to my home?"

"There is no attempt at guilt. I thought you'd want to be here with me."

"That isn't fair, either."

Clay rested his hands on his hips and looked down at the floor as though in deep thought.

"Sophie, if I thought it was in me I'd be begging you to marry me. I care very deeply for you. But I'm not one to settle down with a wife and kids. I'm just like my old man. I've spent my life on the road, never staying in the same place more than a few days, following the rodeo circuit. Since the accident, it's been tough, living here day in and day out. You make it tolerable. I thought you'd like to live here, too."

"I can't, Clay."

"You can't or you won't?"

"Take your choice." She picked up her purse and headed for the door. "I'm taking the afternoon off."

An hour later Sophie was packed and on her way back to the cottage. It felt strange when she entered the modest dwelling. It seemed more small than cozy and she felt very much alone.

She had to admit she missed being around Clay outside of the office setting. His incredible sense of humor kept her laughing in spite of the serious discussion she needed to have with him. But being here, in this house, was better. All she had to do was convince herself she was doing the right thing.

The next morning Clay lost no time in being a total pain in the butt. Even knowing the company was prospering again, he seemed angry, moody and downright offensive to everyone. His short temper wasn't boding well with clients and certainly not with Sophie. His limp was more pronounced. Sophie couldn't help but wonder if it had anything to do with that woman he'd been set to marry, the one who'd dropped him like a hot potato after the accident. Had she called? Had he been using Sophie to forget about that woman? The thought brought immediate pain and she forced it from her mind.

Finally she'd had enough.

"Clay, what's going on?" she asked, standing just inside his office.

"I don't know what you're talking about," he replied without looking directly at her.

"I'm talking about the company. It's prospering again. So what is with the attitude?"

"It's not something I wish to discuss with you. At least not now. See if you can get Greg Johnson on the phone. He withdrew his account and I need to see if I can talk him into coming back on board."

"Right away, *sir*," she replied and turned to head back to her desk.

Was he hurting? It was something he tended to keep hidden away inside, as if it made him less of a man if he admitted to having pain. Totally ridiculous.

The week continued to be tense. Some days Clay would call a halt to business and they both headed to the barn where the horses were saddled and waiting. This was his element. It was where he needed to be. The internal anger disappeared and Clay was at ease with the world.

It was during one of these rides that Sophie was again tempted to tell him about the baby. But she couldn't bring herself to do it. The rare times he was obviously relaxed and happy, she couldn't bring herself to take that away from him. Back in the office, faced with his short temper and foul disposition, she didn't dare.

The following Monday morning, Clay stepped into the office and stopped in front of her desk, a coffee cup in his hand. "Where were you last night? I tried to call but either got a busy signal or your voice mail."

"Then I must have been busy or on the phone." She smiled up at him. It really wasn't any of his business what she did in her own house on her own time. And she certainly didn't owe him any explanation as to whom she was speaking with.

Clay stood there and glared at her for the longest time. Obviously he was trying to make up his mind whether to push it or let it go.

Decision made. "Were you or were you not at home last night?" he barked, as though he had the right to know.

"That really isn't any of your business, Clay. But I'll give you this one—I was at home, on the phone, talking with my mom. My father isn't doing well. He came in from the barn yesterday and he couldn't move his right arm. He complained of a sharp pain in his shoulder. She called for an ambulance right away. Today he will undergo a battery of tests but the general consensus is he had a heart attack. All he could talk about was the pain in his head and shortness of breath. We're currently waiting for the results."

"I'm sorry. Damn, I hope he is okay. I just thought maybe you were—"

"Seeing someone else?" she interrupted. "I'm not. Yet. But you've given me no reason to think I shouldn't go out with someone if asked."

"Sophie, you know I care for you."

"Do I? Just because we had sex does not mean I've assumed it's a monogamous relationship. You've never even hinted at such a thing."

He released a long breath. "Sophie, you know I'm not cut out for marriage. That was proven after I had my accident."

"How? How was it proven? By the fact that selfish woman walked out when you needed her? The fact you were injured? None of it was your fault and you're smart enough to know it. Now, if you're finished prying, I have work to do."

Clay nodded his head and walked to the door. "I hope your dad is okay," he said again. "What is his prognosis?"

Tears immediately flooded her eyes. "Not good. He needs a new heart but he is too old to be put on the list, or so says the doctor."

"How old is he?"

"Sixty-four."

"And they are saying that is too old?" The look

on Clay's face was incredulous. "That's a load of shit. Please keep me informed. If you remember, I met your parents one Christmas. I liked your dad."

"Okay. Thanks." She replied and he disappeared inside of his office.

Clay returned to his office. He might not be able to corral a difficult filly named Sophie, but there was something else he might be able to do. At twelve years old and not a penny to his name, he hadn't been able to save his own father, but maybe... He picked up the phone and contacted the aviation station at the ranch, asking them to ready one of the private plans for immediate departure. Destination: Cleveland, Ohio.

When Sophie arrived at the office the next day, she was surprised to find Clay was not there. A brief, scribbled note said he would be gone for a few days and for her to continue with the basic work. How long was a few days? And what was she going to tell the people who called, given the recent crisis with Everest? She wasted no time picking up the phone and ringing his cell. After several rings, she finally heard his voice on the other end.

"Are you okay?" she asked.

"Yep. Doing fine. Had something I had to take care of. I should be back in Royal sometime tomorrow. If you want, go ahead and forward my calls to the service and take the day off."

"Okay," she said, then disconnected the call. Sophie was puzzled. Normally he told her of any meetings, especially the ones out of town. She shrugged, writing it off to his temperament of late. She straightened her desk and was on her way.

As soon as she walked through her front door, she called the hospital in Indiana only to find her father had been discharged. That should have made her happy but she sensed all was not right. She next called her parents' home. Susan, her younger sister, answered on the fourth ring, her voice sleepy.

"Hey, Susan, it's me. I called the hospital and they told me Dad had been released. Is he at home?"

"No. At least not yet." She yawned. "He was transferred to another hospital. And before you start, I don't know why. You'll have to talk to Mom. She said if you called to tell you not to worry. He was doing better, it's just that they wanted him to see a specialist."

"Is Mom there?"

"No, she's with Dad. She said she would call around noon. If you want, call back this afternoon and I'll tell you what she said."

"I'll just call her myself."

"She won't answer. Something about the hospital rules prevent the use of cell phones in the area he's in. Just call me back this afternoon and I'll tell you what she says."

"Okay. Susan…"

"That's all I know to tell you, Sophie." Another yawn. "Sorry, I was out late last night."

"Well, okay. Sorry I woke you. I'll call later."

"Don't worry about Dad, Soph. He's in good hands."

Susan ended the call.

She would call Susan this afternoon and maybe find out what was going on. Something else… Susan was a bookworm, rarely going out, and even then she was normally home by ten o'clock. Where had she been so late that it would cause her to still be asleep at eleven o'clock in the morning?

That afternoon, before Sophie had a chance to call Susan again, her mom called her.

"We are fine, Sophie," her mom assured her. "Your father is in good hands. He's in the Cleveland Clinic and is undergoing some specialized testing. I'll know more in a week or so and I'll be sure to call."

"Mom? How did you get to Cleveland? Why is Dad there? What specialist is he seeing?"

Before her mother could answer, Sophie heard voices in the background.

"I have to go, sweetheart. Just don't worry. I will

call you immediately if anything bad should happen, but I think it's going to be okay. I love you."

"Love you, too, Mom."

And the call was disconnected, leaving Sophie wondering what was going on and what was it she was not being told?

Thursday morning as Sophie entered the office, she immediately saw Clay behind his desk, reading the morning paper, a cup of coffee in one hand. Approaching, she couldn't help but notice the look of self-satisfaction on his face. Wherever he had been, whatever he'd been doing, he'd apparently been successful. She couldn't help but speculate what it was. He'd probably been signing new accounts for Everest.

"Good morning," she offered. "I'm glad to see you back. Did you have a good outcome to whatever it was you were doing?"

"Good morning," he replied, "and yes, I did. Thank you for asking." The newspaper still blocked his face but by the tone of his voice he'd accomplished what he'd set out to do. Whatever that was.

She went about her business the rest of the day. Clay approached her as she was straightening her desk before going home.

"Can I delay you a few minutes?"

"Sure."

"There is someone I want you to meet."

"Who is it?"

"Come with me and find out."

Together they made their way through the enormous house, out the kitchen door and down a walkway toward the main barn. Bypassing the lobby and the duplicate stalls of horses, Clay continued to the back of the barn, finally stopping in front of a large pen made of solid iron topped by wire panels held together by steel supports.

Sophie peeked through the panels and saw the creature inside. Startled, she jumped back. It was the largest Brahma bull she'd ever seen in her life. She'd guess the weight to be well over a ton.

"Sophie?"

"Not what I was expecting. It's massive! What is a Brahma bull doing here on the ranch?" she asked, her voice quivering. "If that sucker ever got out, it could eat someone's lunch."

Cole smiled and stepped toward the fence. When he held his hand out to Sophie, she hesitantly put her smaller one in his and stepped forward.

"This is Iron Heart. He and I met in a rodeo arena five years ago. And he stomped more than my lunch."

Sophie swallowed hard. "This is the bull that almost killed you?"

Clay silently nodded.

"Clay? What is it doing here?"

"It was scheduled to be euthanized. I found out and had them stop and arranged for him to come here."

"But why?"

"Because that ogre's the only SOB I've ever met who's meaner than me and that deserves some recognition. Besides, he actually saved my life."

"I don't understand."

"If it hadn't been for Iron Heart, I would've entered into a marriage with a woman who I didn't truly love and who certainly didn't love me. It was the roughest damn thing I've ever been through, overcoming both downfalls. But it gave me the chance to build Everest from the ground up into the technology behemoth it is today." He turned to face her. "Just so we're straight, I suffer no regrets that Veronica walked out. None. Not with you beside me."

Sophie was stunned. Not only was Clay showing her a softness he carried inside that hardly anyone ever saw, he was implying…what? That she was the one he really cared for? No. She couldn't read more into his statement then he'd said. She'd simply helped him over the rough spots.

She swallowed hard and stepped back. He had been honest with her. She had so many secrets that she was keeping from him and she had no idea where to start. The full report on the employees at Everest possibly had not included her. But when he found out what she'd done to land her in Texas, it was possible she'd hurt him all over again. He couldn't fall in love with her. He couldn't love a woman who had taken someone's life. She wouldn't allow that to happen.

And then there was the biggest secret of all: she was carrying his baby. She hadn't told him. And at this point she didn't know when she could and delaying telling him was only making it worse.

Clay had opened the gate just a little bit and she stared at the giant in front of her who was contentedly munching on hay. Would Clay be as forgiving with her as he had been with the bull? She doubted it. There was good and there was bad and unlike the bull, she should know the difference.

Sophie didn't know what to say. The bovine death trap standing five feet from her brought back memories. Memories of Clay gasping for another breath. Of his teeth-clenching moans, when he had been unable to keep the pain inside. Of the hours suspended by a breath held in the hope he would live another minute. Of all the tubes, the monitors, the people who'd passed by his bedside with a shake of their heads, silently indicating it was too bad a champion cowboy had almost been killed by the crazy life he'd chosen. Never mind the tickets sold to thousands who had come to watch the event unfold.

She had witnessed it all, never leaving his side. Clay had no one else and because of her own personal circumstances, neither did she. Day after day she wondered where his fiancée was and why she didn't come in to check on him. Finally, during the physical therapy, when Clay needed her the most, the woman had stopped by. Just long enough to watch him struggle onto his feet and leave a message with Sophie along with the five-carat diamond engagement ring. Sophie had sat for days while Clay pushed himself to the limit, holding the ring so tight it cut her palm as she wondered how anyone could do such a thing. She'd prayed for the strength and the words to tell him, inwardly cursing the self-indulgent woman who clearly had no concerns for anyone but herself.

Maybe Clay was right about the bull. Maybe it really had saved his life.

She backed away from the gate, turned and began walking to the front of the barn.

"Sophie!" he called. "Wait up."

She didn't want to wait. She wanted to be a million miles away from here, hidden from the world so she could bear the guilt over her cowardly behavior in secret. It was a mortal sin to take a man's life. It was almost as bad to fall in love with her boss, sleep with him and not tell him she was expecting his child. There was no good end to this. There couldn't be. She didn't want to see the disappointment in his eyes. She didn't want to hear him offer to marry her because it was the honorable thing to do. And Clay, for all his brooding, intimidating persona, was an honorable man.

She had to leave. Even facing the people in her hometown would be better than facing Clay after she told him the truth. And she had to do it before any more time passed.

"Sophie," he called. "Will you wait a second? What's wrong?"

"Nothing," she threw over her shoulder, refusing to slow down. "I've got to get back to the office."

Now she'd added lies to the list. Would the nightmare never end? She had to leave Royal and she had to do it soon.

Nine

Sophie was about to take her bath that evening when her cell rang. Fearing it was Clay, she started to ignore it. She was tired, it had been a long day, and she really didn't want to argue with him any further. But she scooped up the phone and saw it was a call from her mom.

"Hello? Mom?"

"Hi, sweetie. I'm sorry to call so late," her mother said. "But I just wanted to call and let you know that it might be possible for your dad to have an open-heart transplant. Your father is very weak after all the tests and the travel to and from Cleveland, and he had a slight flare-up today. But the doctors say that won't matter once they get the heart. We don't know how long it will be, of course, but we are now on the list. And they'll be able to perform the transplant here at the local hospital—he won't have to go back to Cleveland. Just keep your fingers crossed he can hold on until he gets it."

"Oh, Mom…" The tears blurred Sophie's vision. "That is so great. It's beyond great. But…"

"I know. It's so frightening. But we have…a lot… to be thankful for."

Sophie sat down in a kitchen chair, her own problems suddenly becoming small and unimportant. "Isn't there a specialist he can see? There's got to be someone who can do something."

"Dr. Brixton *is* a specialist, Sophie. Your dad's heart is just worn-out. There are just a lot of people who are in his situation and I guess they feel the younger ones… Well, you know what I'm trying to say."

Yeah, she knew. And while she could see the logic, it was her father who suffered. After the earlier argument with Clay when she refused to move into his house and now this, the whole world seemed to need a redo.

"Mom, I'm coming home."

"Of course, if that's your decision. But I would suggest you wait a while. There is nothing you can do here. As I said, this time he'll be fine. We have been provided a place to stay near the hospital. It's small, but it's a miracle we were able to get it. If you have any vacation, you might want to come back and spend some time with him once he is out of the hospital. If—no, *when*—he gets his new heart, he'll want to spend as much time as he can with both of his girls. I know he would love to see you again. We both would."

"I won't be coming home on vacation leave." She hesitated. "Mom, there is something I need to tell you." Again, she wavered, not really wanting to tell her mother over the phone that she was about to have a grandchild. But she couldn't keep it in any longer. "I'm pregnant."

The silence that hung in the air was not completely unexpected. But she needed her mom. She needed someone she could talk to, someone who would stand up for her and the baby. She knew her mother would be in her corner even if she didn't approve.

Her mother finally said, "Does…does the father know?"

"No." Tears welled in her eyes. "I don't know how to tell him."

"It's important, don't you think?"

"He's not someone who wants to settle down with a family. I'm afraid he may think this is entrapment, an attempt to coerce him into marriage. I don't want a marriage like that. It would never last. Oh, Mom, I love him. But this happened with the wrong guy."

"Sophie, you have to tell him. He has a right to

know." Then she asked the inevitable question. "Is it Clay?"

Sophie's breath left her lungs. "Yes."

"Then, by all means, tell him. He's a good man. You might be surprised by his reaction. But even if you're right, you know we are here for you."

"Thanks. I'll think about what you said and give you a call if I decide to head back to Indiana. Give Dad a big hug and kiss for me, will you?"

When the call ended, she laid her cell on the kitchen table. She had to go home. Her time with Clay was drawing to a close. First, she needed to tell him about her pregnancy and once that information was shared, he would either ask her to leave or she would be so uncomfortable around him she would leave on her own.

Then she needed to return home to be there for her dad. Her family. She could get a call asking her to return home at any time, so she knew she had to tell Clay about the baby even though he wasn't cut out for a relationship, let alone fatherhood. She needed to go back to Indiana so she could be with her family. She had to tell him soon.

"Stay and have supper," Clay said, standing in the open door between their offices the following day. "I'm tired of eating alone."

Sophie eyed him with no small measure of suspicion. There were any number of people he could call on to have supper with. He didn't need her. But maybe it would afford the opportunity to tell him about the baby.

"What are we having?"

"Steaks and baked potato."

"With a salad?"

"Any way you want it."

Clay put in the request and by seven o'clock they were seated outside on the terrace that overlooked land that went on as far as the eye could see. The rolling hills were green—a rarity, happening only in the spring and early summer months. Most of Clay's acreage had been cultivated, seeded each year and fertilized to ensure plenty of grass and forage for the fifty thousand head of cattle that roamed over the land.

"I'm going to ride out to the branding site, probably in the morning. I'm ready to get out of here for a couple of days. I want to see the new calves and get a close-up look at the heifers. We're looking to triple the herd this year and I've decided to add some new bulls to the mix. I need to pick those out, as well." He looked at Sophie. "Want to go?"

"Are you going by horseback?"

"Nah. That would take three days each way. I'll go in the chopper. One day to get there and check everything out, stay overnight to enjoy the campfire and back the next day."

"Okay. Yeah, I'd like to go. How about I have Rose fix some sandwiches and ice down some sodas for the trip?"

"Sounds like a plan."

"When are we leaving?"

"Early."

"How early?"

Clay shrugged. "How about if I wake you just before I'm ready to go?"

"There is a perfectly good alarm clock in my bedroom at the cottage."

"Hell, Sophie. A clock is no way to start the day. There are other things a lot more…invigorating than that."

She picked up her water and took a sip. She knew what he wanted with regard to waking her up. She wanted him, too. But this couldn't go on without her telling him about the life growing inside her. A life he'd helped to create. A little life that might someday have his easy sexy smile and eyes that could melt the coldest heart.

"Name one," she teased.

"Ouch. Now, that hurt."

She set down her glass as Rose came to take away their dinner plates. Sophie then pulled the dish of homemade strawberry shortcake from the center of the table, her mouth already watering.

"Rose is a great cook. But there are some foods

at which she absolutely excels. This is one of them."
Clay picked up his small dessert plate and placed it in front of him, losing no time digging into the tantalizing dessert.

"Oh, my gosh," Sophie said, unable to hold her comment until she'd finished chewing. "This is amazing." She laughed, covering her mouth with her napkin.

For a few minutes neither spoke. The only sound was the clinking of spoons against the bone-china dishes as they inhaled the dessert.

When she was finished, Sophie sipped her water and sat back in the chair, glancing out over the balcony railing at the haunting beauty of the landscape.

The sun was setting, adding a flare of color to the many hills and valleys. It was surreal sitting here with Clay, watching it unfold.

"You are awfully quiet," Clay remarked.

"It's just so stunning. In the five years I've worked for you, I've never taken the time to enjoy the natural wonders of the area. Granted, this balcony provides a perfect place to view it, but I never guessed a dry desert landscape could be so...so..."

"Intriguing?"

"Yes." She smiled. "It really is."

"I love all the old stories about the early gold miners and treasure hunters from the late eighteen hundreds. Many were seen venturing into the mountains with their shovels and gear and never came out. They all wanted to find that illusive treasure said to be left by the early Native Americans or a gold vein found in deep crevices, tunnels and under huge boulders. If you grow up here, as a kid, the talk of finding a treasure or an old map leading to one is a temptation that's hard to ignore."

Sophie couldn't help but laugh. "Are you telling me you used to hunt for buried treasure?"

"Absolutely."

She laughed. "And...were you successful?"

"In a word, no. I found some cave art, which included arrows I swore pointed to the gold. But I never saw one glimmer. Just cactus and rocks."

"I'll bet it was fun to try."

"Yeah, it was."

"This was a great dinner," she said, again looking out to where the last light of the day filtered through the mountains. "Thanks for inviting me. I could sit here and enjoy that view forever."

"So could I," he returned, looking directly at Sophie.

"So you never did answer me seriously," she said. "What time are we leaving?"

"I was serious about waking you but okay, if you'd rather use an alarm, set it for six."

"Done. This is going to be fun."

With Clay at the controls, the helicopter left the ground heading west. It rose to a height that still allowed them to see the terrain and watch it change from green grass and towering pines to red rocks, cactus and sage. Then back up and over a mountain pass to find pine and oak trees again. They flew over valleys, saw rivers and tributaries as the water flowed at the bottom of deeply cut gorges and into green valleys. But even though the desert was sparse by comparison to the green mountain peaks, it had a romantic draw all its own.

All too soon the cattle and the cowboys who herded them began to appear. It looked like a massive undertaking.

"They bring them all into camp and sort them by sex and age," Clay said over the headset. "The younger ones receive our brand. The two-year-old bulls are what I came to see. I want to add about fifty to the breeding plan. The rest will be taken to market."

A few minutes later, Clay set the chopper down near what appeared to be the central branding operation. White pipe and steel fencing held hundreds of cattle, with more on the way. Together he and Sophie exited the helicopter and walked toward the center of the operation. Clay approached two men standing at the fence. Handshakes and greetings were exchanged, and Clay introduced them to Sophie. Then he lost himself in a discussion of the two-year-old bulls and Sophie was glad to stand back and watch. He was in his element. How he managed to pull on a suit and tie and look like a businessman, convincing people who didn't know him he'd just walked off Wall Street, she didn't know. This was the real Clay: all about horses and cattle and working the land. More comfortable on a green-broke horse than in a limo.

Around one o'clock, Clay reappeared and found his way to where she sat near a huge campfire. "How about some lunch?"

"Sounds good to me."

They walked back to the chopper and Clay hoisted the woven basket Rose had prepared for them from the back.

"I wonder what Rose sent."

"I don't know but it will be delicious whatever it is," she said.

"How about we go over there next to the river. I see a flat rock in the shade."

"Perfect."

The basket contained a variety of sandwiches, salads and several slices of apple pie for desert. "I'll bet those treasure hunters you were talking about would have given anything to have had Rose in their corner."

Clay chuckled. "No doubt."

The stillness of the day was not missed by Sophie. It was early enough in the year that the soaring heat of summer usually made trips such as this unbearable. But not today. In the far distance a bird sang to its mate, and cows bellowed their dislike at having their peaceful day interrupted. The water in the river ran over the stones and small boulders, giving a serene sound to the tranquil setting.

"Did you fly out and see a lot of the land before you bought it?"

"Somewhat. I didn't have time to view all twenty-two thousand acres, but enough that I knew I wanted to invest. I've always been fascinated by the desert. Plus this parcel had the added benefit of the mountains covered in the ponderosa pines. The best of both worlds. I was lucky I found it."

"That was back when you were still following the rodeo circuit?"

"Yeah. I wanted to build the barns and an arena and hold semiannual livestock shows and rodeos closer to the house."

"You still can," she said matter-of-factly, folding her sandwich bag and grabbing a piece of the pie. "You have the barn. All you need is the main arena."

Clay nodded. "I may still do it someday. Right now I have to battle what's going on in corporate America. That, I've learned, is a whole different world."

"Well, I hope someday you pursue your dream." She bit into the piece of apple pie. "It would be a shame if you don't. You certainly earned it." The instant she said it, she realized she wouldn't be there to see it and that brought a wave of sadness that gripped her heart. She would be back in Indiana, teaching school or tutoring children to earn her way. That was if—big if—the local school officials would hire her after the barn-burning incident. It was a small community. Even smaller than Royal. People had a way of remembering everything.

"Sophie?"

"I'm here," she said, forcing herself out of the sad thoughts and giving him what she hoped was a bright smile. "Just taking in everything I've seen today. It's so massive an undertaking. So many cattle and cowboys."

"It's hard work," Clay agreed. "I did it for years in between hitting the rodeos. In the early days it was how I managed to pay for attending a rodeo. Eventually I was making more riding bulls than I ever made working on a ranch. A lot of these guys—" he nodded toward the ranch hands bringing in the next lot of cattle "—will be the next Trevor Brazile or Tye Murray."

"Or Clay Prescott," she added.

"Yeah, I hope they find a way to end their career a little better than I did."

"Excuse me, Clay?" A tall, lean cowboy stood before them. "Sorry to bother but we've got about three hundred two-year-olds in the holding pens if you want to take a look at them. It's getting kind of full and there are more on the way."

"Absolutely," Clay said, getting to his feet. "Sophie, want to come?"

"Sure. Go ahead. I'll pack up the scraps and join you."

The afternoon went fast. Sophie was mesmerized by the newborn calves and spent much of her time with her camera taking pictures of their antics. Running and challenging each other, they were preparing for adulthood even though they were only a few weeks old. Their mothers grazed near them as though they had no cares in the world. Until the calves got too far away.

Dinner around the huge campfire was a meal of chili and corn muffins and beer to wash it all down. As with dinner last night, Sophie stuck to water. She assumed after eating they would head back to the homestead and was surprised to learn they weren't leaving until morning. They had brought no sleeping bags and she doubted they could sleep in the chopper. But after dinner that was exactly where they headed: back to the helicopter.

"Clay, can't we just go home? I don't know about sleeping in this thing."

He chuckled. "We're not sleeping in this. We're using it to go about two miles away to a hunting cabin. With the mountains and changes in altitude, I don't like to fly at night in this area. Don't worry, it's not very big but you'll be comfortable."

"Okay. If you say so."

Ten

They lifted off and headed east, following a tree line that could still be seen in the growing darkness below. They came to a large flat bolder on the edge of the towering pines and Clay landed. There was a small path that disappeared into the heavy growth of trees.

"Come on. Let's get there before it grows any darker." He held out his hand and she grabbed it. The path was wide enough that they could walk side-by-side. Clay's right hand rested on her lower back as he guided her through the forest. Finally, up ahead, she saw lights.

The hunting lodge was no shack. In fact, it was a

spin-off of the mansion at the home site as far as architectural design. Log walls extended up and disappeared into the surrounding trees. There was a warm, welcoming glow from the huge floor-to-ceiling windows. They stepped across a wide porch and Clay opened the door for her, encouraging her to go inside. She found herself a large main room with a kitchen located behind it and stairs on the right.

"The second story isn't finished yet," he explained. "But this sofa turns into a bed and there are sleeping bags, blankets and pillows stored in the closet. You take the bed. I'll bunk down on the floor. Are you hungry?"

"No, thank you," she said as she placed a hand over her stomach. "That chili was so good I ate like a pig. Who makes it anyway?"

"I think this year it was a team effort."

"They did good." She smiled.

"Would you like a fire?"

She shook her head, "That's okay. It's too much trouble to go to for just one night."

"It's not a problem."

Sophie longingly glanced over at the large stone fireplace. It reminded her of her home back in Indiana. She'd spent a good part of her early years in front of a warming fire. The longing must have shown on her face.

"The wood is already chopped and corded right

outside. It's no problem. A fire sounds good. Make yourself at home."

Clay stopped with his hand on the doorknob. From the soft glow coming from the kitchen area, she watched his eyes as he scanned her face, his expression a mixture of concern and complacency and something else she couldn't quite put a finger on. They were large, intelligent eyes, the color of the dark moss that grew on the rocks and seriously intense. His lips were full and sensuous. Her breathing all but stopped. Then he pulled open the door. "I'll be back in a couple of minutes. The bathroom is there." He indicated the door behind the sofa. "There are fresh towels and soap. Use whatever you need."

She glanced in the direction he'd indicated and nodded.

Although sparse, the room was decorated in a theme that complemented the terrain surrounding the cabin. She walked to the bathroom and was surprised by the size. It was a large space with both a deep tub and a shower. It didn't take her long to draw hot water into the tub. Soon she'd removed her clothes and stepped into the deep, warm water. Looking up, she saw they had a skylight. This would be a remarkable cabin when it was finished. With a sigh she opened a bottle of the sage-scented shampoo she'd found in a cabinet next to the sink and lost herself in the comforting warmth of the bath.

She had expected Clay to tap on the bathroom door after finding some reason to come inside. She was ready for him. She had her no practiced and on the tip of her tongue. But there was no knock, only the sound of owls calling to each other outside the cabin.

True to his word, Clay had converted the sofa into a bed with extra blankets and pillows when she finally did step out of the bathroom. The kindling in place, all it took was one flick of the lighter and soon a small fire was blazing in the fireplace, its flames sending warmth into the room. As it snapped and crackled in the hearth, Sophie was drawn to it like a moth to a light. There was just something about a warm fire and the smell of burning wood she had always loved. Wrapped in a fluffy white bathrobe, she sat down and ran a brush through her hair, stroke after stroke. It wouldn't take long to dry in front of the fireplace.

Clay opened the door and walked inside with one more stack of wood. After dropping the logs near the hearth, he stopped and watched her hair-drying process. He had the urge to kiss her, to feel those sumptuous lips against his just once more. He knew that would be a mistake. She'd been through a lot today. She was tired and more than likely sex was the furthest thing from her mind. He needed to give her the respect she was due and remember she was here to see the cattle drive. She needed to feel safe without any fear of him jumping her bones.

But damn. She'd felt so right in his arms. And in such close proximity, without any substantial clothing to shield her from his touch, he'd been painfully aware of each and every curve of her body. Of the smooth softness of her skin and the silkiness of her hair. Even after the day she'd had, she smelled good, like an herb garden with some dandelions thrown in for good measure. He didn't want or need any personal relationships to complicate a life that had already gone off the deep end thanks to a bull and some degenerate determined to bring Everest down. All the more reason to get her back to where she needed to be as soon as possible. Keep the perspective, he thought. It was only one night.

Holy mother of God. He was in for a long night.

"If this sofa is your only bed, then you sleep here. I'll take the floor." It was the least she could do.

"You're fine."

"But I don't want to take your bed."

"Don't worry about it," he replied as he stretched out on the blanket. "Of course, we could always share. Then both of us would be warm and comfy."

"I'll keep that in mind," she said as she reached over and turned off the small lamp next to the sofa.

Sophie lay down, surprised the bed was as soft

and comfortable as it was. She adjusted the pillow and pulled the covers over her. Staring at the ceiling, she watched the shadows created by the flames as they danced over the burning logs. The fire gave out so much warmth, soon she felt too warm. She kicked her way out from under the cover, but the room still felt hot. Water. She needed a drink of cool water. She pushed to her feet, stepped over his legs and entered the kitchen. After opening and closing several cabinets, she finally located the glasses. Next she moved to the sink, ran some water then filled the glass.

"Is there a problem?" he called from the other room.

"Just getting a glass of water," she answered. "Do you want some?"

"No, thanks."

"It's good. Sometimes water from a well tastes… coppery. Bitter. But this is really good."

"I am so glad you like it."

Was that a sarcastic remark? It was hard to judge because she really didn't know his current mood. The day's outing could have hurt his bad leg. Deciding to let it drop, she finished drinking the water then turned on the tap and rinsed her glass before returning it to the cabinet. Once she'd stepped back over his feet, she returned to the couch and laid down.

The wind had picked up and it whistled around the corner of the cabin. Then all was quiet. She settled back and took a deep breath. Suddenly another gust of wind blew against the outside door. It sounded as though it had partially blown open. Had he remembered to securely close and lock it when he came in? He'd had his hands full of split logs. Maybe he'd forgotten. Another few minutes of speculation and she threw the blanket off and stood up from the couch. Stepping over his legs, she walked to the door, pushed against it and locked it.

"What are you doing?"

"I was afraid you'd forgotten to lock the door."

"And you're concerned someone might stroll by and break in?"

"It could happen."

To that he made no comment. Well, she would make sure they slept in safety, even if he was not concerned. She stepped back over his legs, then plopped down on the sofa bed and pulled the blanket over her. It took quite a few punches at the pillow before it finally formed a position she deemed comfortable. She wondered what time it was. Probably around midnight. She didn't have her watch.

Sitting up, she glanced around the room. On the wall over the bar there appeared to be a clock, but she couldn't make out the time. Throwing off the blanket, she stood up, again stepped over Clay's feet and made her way around the counter. It was a clock. But it wasn't light enough in the room to read the time.

Feeling her way around the walls of the small area, she tried to find a light switch. No go. She didn't know where he'd put his flashlight. Would he have a lighter? Or some matches? She turned and began to open the drawers, her hands searching inside for a box of matches.

"Sophie…?"

"I… I'm looking for some matches."

"Why do you need matches?"

"To see the clock."

"Why do you want to see the clock?"

"Well, duh. I'd like to know what time it is."

She heard him mutter some foul things under his breath then there was a slight rustling of covers. "It's one-fifteen. Now could we please try and get some sleep?"

"Yeah. Sorry."

She stepped over him and sat down on the sofa, wishing she were sleepy. "Are you in pain or are you always this grumpy?"

"Yes. I'm often grumpy. As you well know."

She turned on her side, facing the fire, and closed her eyes. She wasn't used to sleeping in strange surroundings. The sun came up around seven o'clock this time of year. A few more hours and she could get back to the ranch and on to her own cozy cottage.

Eventually she was able to ignore the unfamiliar sounds, stopped worrying about the door blowing open and found a position under the blanket that was neither too hot nor too cool. The tranquility of the night surrounded her and she slept.

Sophie didn't know if it was a scream or a growl or something in between that yanked her out of a deep sleep. But it was loud. Whatever made the noise was right outside and it didn't sound happy. She pulled the blanket up to her nose and hardly dared to breath. All was still. Had she imagined it?

Just about the time she began to relax, it happened again. This time the loud, long, screaming growl made the hair on the back of her neck stand straight up. Without giving a second thought to her actions, she sprang from the sofa. Her feet caught in the blanket, and before she could catch herself, she fell, landing squarely on top of Clay.

She heard him make an *ugh* sound. In less than a heartbeat, she was flat on her back, his massive body above her, holding her in place. One large hand roughly gripped her shoulder while the other hand held a gun, cocked and aimed directly at the door. For a long moment, they regarded each other through the darkness. She heard the click-click of a trigger being released. At least, she hoped that was what it was.

"What in the hell are you doing?" His voice was low and menacing, obviously angry, but he loosened his grip.

"I… It… The sound. Something right outside… screamed. You didn't hear it?"

Taking in a deep breath, he seemed to be gathering his patience. "It was a cat. A cougar. I told you they roam this area. They can't get inside, so you're perfectly safe."

"I'm glad I locked the door," she mumbled.

"So am I. He could have pulled out his key and walked in."

There was that tone again.

"I didn't know…about the cougar," she whispered, her gaze focused on the depths of his eyes through the fire's glow. "I've never experienced anything like that."

He didn't move, didn't say anything more. His thumb began to softly caress the side of her neck as his eyes held hers. It was as though in his mind he was making a decision.

"Clay… I didn't mean to—"

He lowered his head and his lips covered hers. Sophie was struck by the soft, pliability of his mouth, warm, gentle, enticing, which was a complete contrast to the hard-muscled body that partially covered hers. His tongue drew across her lips, coaxing them to open. Without conscious thought, she complied. With a moan he filled her mouth, going deep, as though he needed to taste all she had to offer. Sophie had never been kissed like this even by Clay, with such expertise, such blatant sexuality. It was animal. It was wild. It was so far removed from the stilted good-night kisses she'd experienced the few times she'd gone out on dates with other men. But this...this was a kiss. He tasted like coffee and his own unique all-male flavor. Too soon, his lips left hers as he licked and kissed across her jaw and down her neck. His hot breath was against her ear, causing delicious shivers to dance across her skin. His mouth returned to hers and she was once again sinking in a dizzying storm of emotions as his mouth, his scent, the feel of his skin and the power of his body consumed all rational thoughts.

Suddenly, Clay broke off the kiss.

"Sophie, make no mistake. I want you so badly it hurts. I want to take you over and over again, but I can't make any promises beyond tonight."

She let her eyes roam over the handsome face, eventually coming to rest on his full lips. "No requests for any promises."

"God, Sophie."

Clay made a slight adjustment and she felt his desire pressing against her core. Her body's natural instinct was to push against him. In response, he moaned, low and deep. His lips again covered hers in another deep, drugging kiss, laced with pure fire.

Sophie knew they were about to cross the line. Again. One that seemed to be growing thinner by the second. If she didn't say no right now, she knew she was going to let Clay make love to her. He was going to shatter the fragile facade they had both tried to maintain since he'd made love to her the last time.

As if sensing apprehension, he raised his head, watching her through the dim glow of the fire, his eyes almost black with desire. Her gaze moved over his face, finally coming to rest on his mouth.

"I'm in love with you." The words tumbled out of her mouth before she could catch them. She ran one finger across his bottom lip and felt his manhood expand even more against her.

He lightly bit the tip of her finger before sucking it gently into his mouth. His tongue teased the nerve endings before he released it. A shot of singeing heat speared through her.

In what seemed to be slow motion, his lips again descended on hers, his mouth more gentle than before. His hands cupped her head in a firm embrace, as though holding her where she needed to be. She inhaled the raw scent of pure male, lost in the heady potency that surrounded him. She felt her body relax, her mind clear of all doubts, accepting what was to come without any thought of denying him what she knew he was about to take. The breath left her lungs on a sigh as the world grew hazy and she knew heaven on earth.

One hand left her head and moved down her body, inching her panties down over her hips and off her feet. Then his hand was there, testing her heat and ensuring she was ready to take him. One finger disappeared inside her and Sophie moaned her delight. She pressed against his hand as though driven to do so with no rational thought of her own. With a slight adjustment, his hand left her and his mouth took its place, his tongue pushing in deep.

She heard him growl as he continued to enjoy the silken flesh. She couldn't feel any more, her mind going numb as her body exploded. Then he was pushing inside her, kissing her deeply, moving his lean, muscular body over hers.

The air around them became singed with the heat from their bodies as Clay continued to move. His mouth was joined to hers as though they were two parts of a whole, his tongue filling her, mimicking the movements of his lower body. Sophie was lost. She could only feel and the feelings were incredible. Of their own accord her legs lifted to surround his back as Clay pushed deeper. Then, with one final push, Sophie exploded. Stars surrounded her as she floated somewhere between heaven and Clay's touch. Then he joined her and she held him tight against her.

When it was over, he dropped down next to her, breathing deep, matching her own gasps for air.

"You're incredible," he murmured against her ear.

"Clay?"

"Hmm?"

"I'm also…pregnant."

Eleven

Everything stopped.

Clay froze as though caught in an electric fence, his body paralyzed. He dropped his head onto her chest, still breathing hard. Her hands automatically reached for him, her fingers threading through his hair.

In a few seconds he raised his head and looked at her through the semidarkness. "Are you sure?"

"Yes." She nodded. "I've seen a doctor. The best I can figure is it happened in May after the masked charity ball."

He frowned. "How long have you known?"

"For sure…about four weeks. I… I didn't know how to tell you."

"Oh, Sophie." His long fingers ran down the side of her face. "You are full of surprises."

"I don't want anything from you, Clay," she hurried to explain. "I certainly didn't get this way on purpose. Hopefully, you know that."

"I believe you, Sophie. If the baby is mine, I'll take care of it. Of both of you."

If the baby is mine? What did he mean by that?

"*If* the baby is yours? Who else would be the father?" She pushed against his shoulders and he dropped to one side of her.

"Don't take that the wrong way. It didn't come out the way I meant."

"Oh, gosh. I understand," she quipped as she struggled to get out of the sleeping bag. "I guess you found out about all those other guys I've been with since May," she spat out sarcastically. "Oops."

"That isn't what I meant," he said.

"I don't need anyone to take care of us, and unless you believe in modern-day immaculate conception, I assure you this baby is yours. Let me up."

He immediately withdrew his muscled legs from over hers and she pushed to her feet.

"What are you doing?"

"I'm going home."

She headed for the sofa, stubbing her little toe on its leg. In the semi-dark, she groped for her jeans and her shirt.

"And just how are you going to do that?"

"What do you mean, how am I...?"

"Sophie, we'll go home first thing in the morning, as soon as it's light. Now come back over here and let me keep you warm."

For a few long moments she sat on the couch, shivering. She didn't want anything from him, including his warmth. But she had to think of the baby. Muttering, she limped back to the sleeping bag and got inside. His arm came around her, bringing with it the heat from his large frame.

"You're shivering," he said as he pulled her closer, his powerful leg again draping over hers. "You know what? Roll over on your side. If we spoon, I can keep you warmer."

Sophie released an aggravated sigh and did as he asked. Did he really think the baby wasn't his? How could he think that? He knew the hours she kept. If she'd been going out on a date, he would know it.

"I didn't mean that the way it sounded," Clay whispered, as if he could read her mind. His right hand rested against her stomach. After a few silent minutes, he asked, "Is it a boy or a girl?"

"It's too soon to tell."

"Hmm." And with that he laid his head down on the shared pillow.

Sophie didn't move. Clay hadn't yelled at her or gotten mad; his surprise was a given. But he seemed to accept it. So far. In fact, he'd accepted it a lot better than she'd thought he would. Not that he had a lot of choice. She hadn't meant to blurt it out, especially at the time she did. She had just been caught up in the overpowering love she had for him.

What would he do now? Would his mood change in the morning? And how should she handle it either way? Sadly, in part because of his comment, the thought crossed her mind again that her time with Clay might be drawing to a close. She fully intended to go back home to Indiana and give her mom what support she could. Would Clay care one way or another, aside from the fact that he'd be losing a good assistant? That was very sad. At least he hadn't denied it was his. And now he knew, so perhaps the worst was over. Tomorrow or the next day she would have to tell him she was leaving. She hoped the news would bring as much acceptance and understanding as learning he was about to be a father. But somehow, she doubted it. She closed her eyes and a tear rolled down her cheek. Maybe things would look better in the morning.

"Sophie," Clay called to her. She shook her head, not wanting to talk.

"Sophie, I need you to look at me," he persisted. "Come on, honey."

She moaned her unwillingness and tried to recapture that plateau, that heady ambience she only felt in Clay's arms.

"Come on, darlin'." Slowly her eyelids parted, as her mind struggled to do as he asked.

"Hey, there you are." He smiled.

Her gaze was rooted to his mouth. Those lips. Her arms reached up, over his shoulders. Her fingers felt the short hair at the back of his head as she pulled his mouth down to hers. He kissed her long and deep then placed a quick kiss on her forehead and sat back. She noticed he was no longer inside the sleeping bag. In fact, he was dressed and ready for the day.

"Come on, Sophie. Wake up. It's morning. We need to be on our way back to the ranch."

She eyed him from inside the sleeping bag. The events of the night trickled over her like cold running water. Was he angry? Upset? She couldn't immediately tell. He hadn't given her the impression he was angry last night when she'd told him about the baby. Surprised, yes. But not mad.

She would wait, she decided, before she broached the subject again, wait until he'd had time to digest the news and then ask how he felt about it. She hoped he would want to be a part of the baby's life but she wasn't holding her breath. She couldn't let go of a bit of disappointment that he'd not been happy at the news. While maybe it was unrealistic, she had hoped he would at least be joyful. Maybe not ecstatic, but a bit excited. Apparently not.

The trip back to the ranch was unusually quiet. Clay was absorbed by the information Sophie had laid on his doorstep. She was having his child. He had no doubt it was his. She didn't date, although why a beautiful woman like Sophie would remain almost celibate he couldn't begin to guess. As close as they were, he would certainly know if there was another man in the picture.

She'd said she loved him. He'd taken it as something she might say in the heat of passion. Could she truly feel that way? And if so, where did that leave him? He certainly cared for Sophie. Deeply. She was his best friend and a very special person in his life, a life that wouldn't be the same without her in it. But he didn't know if he loved her. He wasn't sure he knew what love was.

Was it a son or a daughter? Either option filled him with a pride such as he'd never felt. He could hand off the reins to his corporations to either one when he decided to retire. No more worries about that. But that was assuming Sophie didn't take the child and return to Indiana. He refused to seriously believe she would do that because, dammit, he didn't want to believe it. Through the years of physical therapy and working side by side, she'd come to mean a lot to him. But a wife…? He had never seen himself as the type of man who would settle down with a family. He still didn't. He needed to make sure she knew he was excited about the baby without giving the impression that he was ready to put a ring on her finger. But his conscience kept hammering the point home: *You know it's the right thing to do.*

He would give Sophie the choice.

He flew a semicircle around the ranch grounds before setting the helicopter down on the tarmac next to the others. A car was waiting to take them to the house.

"Have dinner with me tonight?" he asked as they approached the car. "I think we need to talk."

She hesitated. "All right."

"I'll pick you up around eight?"

She nodded.

"In fact, let me take you home. You must be exhausted."

She stopped. "Why would I be exhausted?"

"It was a long trip. And in your condition…"

"What? My condition makes me lazy?"

"You said that, not me."

"So? It's what you were thinking." She made a scoffing sound and turned toward her car.

"How, um, how did you arrive at that determination?" He had to get a grip on this. She was picking fights, objecting to anything he said. That was not what he'd meant but he'd be damned if he would follow her around and keep apologizing.

"Don't worry about it," she threw over her shoulder. "And forget dinner. You're right. I'm just too tired and lazy to make the effort."

"Sophie. Stop."

She stopped.

"Look, I might not have handled this right from the beginning. I get that telling a guy you are having his child is supposed to be a romantic moment. You just caught me off guard. Actually, you blew my mind is what you did. But I do respect you. I do know, without any doubt, that it's my baby. And the more time I have to let it soak in, the more I'm realizing I'm kinda happy about it."

"Really?" Hope mixed with surprise in her voice.

"Really. Look, why don't you stay here instead of going home? We can have an early dinner—or a late one. Whichever you prefer. I need to go into the office and check things out. One of your old swimsuits is upstairs, in that first small room on the right as you go up the main staircase. Remember, you used to use it for a changing room? Just swim, relax—that's *not* calling you lazy. Or, if you want, walk with me inside to the office."

"I… I would actually like that."

"Come on, then."

Together they walked inside the enormous home

and turned toward the wing that had been designated as office space. While he returned phone calls, Sophie went through the foot-thick stack of mail.

The office phones weren't usually answered on Sundays. It was with surprise that Clay noticed the solid white light on one of the secondary lines on his phone. After ending his call, he couldn't help but speculate about who Sophie was speaking to. Before he could walk over to the connecting door, the volume of her voice increased.

"So you're saying they have a heart?"

She was quiet while she listened to the answer.

"Oh, Mom. Call me when it's over. Please."

Another silence. A sniff. Was Sophie crying?

"Okay. Mom, I'll keep my cell with me. Call as soon as you know?"

Silence.

"I will. Mom, I'm coming home. It should be in about two weeks, sooner if I can make it happen."

Quiet.

"I know. I know." There was a pause. "Okay, Mom. I'll talk with you soon. Bye."

"Sophie?" Clay called to her as he walked through their door. "Is everything all right?"

"As I told you, Dad is sick. But they may have found him a heart. He is really weak, but the heart is in transport, so..." The tears filled her eyes. "He has a chance."

Clay walked to where she was sitting, still holding her cell phone. "That's great." He reached out and covered her hands with hers. "Did I tell you my dad died of a heart attack?"

"No. You've never mentioned him."

Clay pulled up a chair. "I was twelve. I knew he was sick but at the time I never fully understood what it meant. Back then transplants weren't as common as they are today." He shrugged. "Anyway, he was out branding steers and just clutched his chest and fell over."

"Oh, Clay, I'm so sorry."

"Thanks. Did I hear you were planning on going home?"

"Yes, I need to return home to Indiana. I'll write out my resignation tomorrow. I need to be packed and on my way as soon as I can arrange it."

"You're leaving permanently?"

"Yes."

"Sophie, why don't you take some time off, return to your parents' home and see how things pan out? Take as long as you need. Just don't leave with the intention of never coming back."

She was quiet for a long time. Clay had to wonder if it was strictly because of her dad's illness or if the baby had something to do with it. She was going to have a baby. He hadn't committed to anything but supporting her monetarily. He could do that from anywhere. Did she think he was trying to pay her off? Did she think he wouldn't be there for both her and the baby? Was she using any of it as an excuse to leave her job, to make a clean break with Everest? Or was it Clay Everett she needed to get away from?

"I don't know at this point when I might be able to come back. If…if something happens to Dad, Mom will need me there. Yes, my older sister, Susan, is there, but frankly she isn't all that dependable. She means well but… I just don't know, Clay."

He needed to get a grip on this.

"So, you're saying you plan to give birth to our baby in Indiana? Will I be notified when the event occurs?" He couldn't keep the sarcasm out of his voice.

"Of course. You'll get plenty of notice if I can reach you. If that's what you want."

"If that's what I want? Sophie… Have dinner with me tonight," he said. "Give us a chance to talk this out. You told me about the baby less than twenty-four hours ago. It hasn't been long enough to really soak in let alone realize what I need to do."

She smiled. "Clay, you don't *need* to do anything. You've been through so much in the past several years. And now you're dealing with some creep spreading rumors about Everest and it's causing you greater stress and worry. I don't want to cause you any more."

"Sophie…"

"I've got to go home. I want to call Mom again and get the latest news on Dad. I'll see you tomorrow. We can talk in the office about anything you feel is necessary."

With that she picked up her small overnight case and her purse and headed to the door of the office. "I enjoyed this weekend. Thanks for taking me along. Sorry I had to go and spoil it."

Clay watched from the window as she went outside and walked to where her car was parked. With one last wave, she backed out of the parking space and headed for the road that would take her back to the cottage.

Clay wasn't in the office Monday morning. It was a first for him, but not really all that surprising considering what she'd dropped on him over the weekend. She thought she would hear from him but apparently not. What did that mean? She had no clue. Part of her said she was exactly where she thought she would be with regard to their relationship. He'd taken the news of the pending birth in stride, just like he did everything else. He'd accepted it, hadn't questioned if the child was his, and life went on. She knew better than to expect emotion; still, she was slightly disappointed. But she reminded herself that it could've been much worse.

The office phones began to ring, indicating a typically busy start to a Monday morning. She had told him she would work another two weeks, not wanting to leave him shorthanded even though he had plenty of secretaries he could get here at a moment's notice. She put in a call to the home office's human-resources department and requested the same two secretaries who'd helped them out before when they were dealing with the Everest PR crisis. They had already been trained on the basic office procedures and would be able to step in without any problems. They would start the following Monday.

When she contacted her mother after getting back to the cottage on Sunday afternoon, it had come as a relief to hear the smile in her mother's voice. Everything had been arranged. Her father was to have the heart transplant on Wednesday. The prognosis was good. She let her mom know she had given her notice and would be coming back to Indiana. She'd call her again when she had a definite time of arrival.

Sophie got up and walked to the large picture window in her office. It looked out over the distant barns, forest and to the right the miles and miles of open range. She would miss this. She would miss working for Clay. This job, and Clay, had become her life. She spent more time in this office and with him than she did in her cottage. Maybe she and the baby could come back to visit in the future. She'd also made friends with a lot of the ranch hands and their families who lived on the spread. She knew when they found out she was pregnant they would want to see the baby. But she wasn't the kind of person to pick up the phone and tell someone. At least not until Clay had made his intentions perfectly clear. For all she knew, he might not want anyone to know he was about to become a father. As these were his employees, she would leave it to him to tell them or not.

It was sad when she realized the greatest joy in her life was one she had to keep to herself. Maybe Clay would come around. He might not want to raise the baby under his roof, but at least her pregnancy would serve as no embarrassment to him. Miracles were in short supply this year and she had given her allotment to her dad.

Twelve

Friday morning as Sophie entered the office, she immediately saw Clay behind his desk, hiding behind his newspaper as usual.

"Good morning," she offered. "I'm glad to see you back. I hope you enjoyed your vacation."

"I did."

"Well, when you decide to go to work, there are several calls you need to make. The messages are all on your desk and in the order you need to return them."

"How are you feeling?"

His question surprised her. "Good. Well. Thank you. Still having the morning sickness but I should be through it soon. It usually goes away by the second trimester."

That brought the newspaper down as he looked at her carefully. "I hadn't realized you'd been sick. I'm sorry. Is there anything I can do?"

"Nope. It's just part of being pregnant."

He rose from his chair and walked to her. Catching her chin with his fingers, he raised her face to his. In what seemed like slow motion, he lowered his lips to hers. "I want to be with you through this, Sophie. I want to be there for you to ensure anything you need is at your disposal. I want you to marry me, Sophie. I realize this isn't the way things should've gone down. This is neither the place nor the time to ask for your hand in marriage but I want to take care of you and I want to take care of our son or daughter."

"You don't have to be married to take care of your son or your daughter. As I said before, I don't really want anything from you. Don't feel you are required to give up your freedom simply because I got pregnant."

Inside, Sophie's heart was beating hard against her chest. She couldn't deny to herself how badly she wanted to tell him yes. She wished this would turn out differently. Yes, she wanted to marry Clay. She wanted to be his wife in every sense of the word. She wanted them to be a family and live on the ranch. But she'd realized long ago people didn't always get what they wanted. She knew he loved her in his own way but that wasn't enough. Being her best friend did not make him husband material.

"Make those calls," she said as she left his office for her own. "They're important."

Sophie glanced at her watch. It was almost ten o'clock. She needed to drive down to the local bank and Clay's attorney's to pick up the documents he needed to sign pertaining to Everest's corporate restructuring. She pressed the intercom. "I've got to run to the bank. Anything you need me to get while I'm in town?"

"No, thanks."

The drive from the ranch into downtown Royal took about twenty minutes. First National Bank of Royal was located on Main Street. Clay's attorney had an office on the second floor. After stopping into the bank, Sophie headed upstairs. Mary Sue, the legal secretary, was waiting for her when she stepped off the elevator.

"Did you come to pick up those papers on the Everest reorganization?"

"Yep."

"I have them ready for you right over here."

Sophie followed Mary Sue to a side table with a large stack of paperwork. She placed them in manila envelopes and handed them to Sophie.

"Have you heard Joe Croswell's business was targeted by what sounds like the same idiot who tried to bring Everest down?"

"No, I didn't know. That person has got to be caught and stopped."

"I don't think you'll find anyone in this town who would disagree with you there."

"Well, thanks for the paperwork. I'll get it to Clay right away."

After a few more parting words, Sophie made her way out of the bank to her car and headed back to the ranch. As she drove, she contemplated Maverick. She couldn't understand anyone who had so much hatred that they'd try to bring down every business in Royal. But she wouldn't have to worry about it anymore. Clay had overcome the crisis directed at his company; plus, she would be leaving next week.

She'd made quite a few friends here over the past five years and while she didn't want to tell people she was leaving for fear of being asked why, she would miss them nonetheless. She hoped their friendship could continue on a long-distance basis.

Once she parked her car in her assigned space, she grabbed the envelope in her purse and hurried inside. Clay's door was closed, which was unusual unless something was very wrong, but she certainly would respect his privacy. Before she could speculate further, her own phone began to ring. Grabbing the cell phone from her purse, she saw that it was a text from Clay telling her to please return to his office as soon as possible.

Was it possible that Clay had made a decision? Had he finally decided he wanted to be the baby's father and a true husband to her? Could he have meant it when he'd ask her to marry him? They way he'd said he wanted to take care of her and their baby made it sound like the marriage offer was responsibility talking. Not love. Not a desire to be with her. Had she been wrong? Hope filled her heart as she walked to the closed door. Maybe he would even forgive her when he found out about her past. It hit her with the velocity of a freight train that there was nothing she wanted more. With those thoughts in mind, she knocked twice on Clay's office door, then she opened it as she had done for years and stepped inside. Only this time Clay wasn't by himself. Behind his desk—on his lap—was a beautiful blonde woman, her long hair touching her waist as she laughed at something that had just been said. After the initial shock, Sophie couldn't help but notice the woman sat straddling Clay's lap, her short skirt riding up almost to her panty line. Clay's hands were around her waist and his face was covered in lipstick. Sophie could feel the blood drain from her face as she mumbled an apology and backed out of the room.

She knew the woman. She was one of Clay's mistresses before he had his accident, before he'd become engaged. Carla. Her name was Carla something.

Tears stung Sophie's eyes as she stumbled over the

legs of her chair. Apparently, he couldn't even wait until she'd left to carry on with his numerous affairs. It smacked of arrogance and the disdain he apparently had for her and their unborn child. After she'd grabbed her purse from under the desk, she ran for the outside door. But when she got inside her car, the engine wouldn't start. Numbed, she looked around hoping a solution would fall into her lap. It did. Jesse May Holbrook came through the gate that connected the estate grounds with the barn and surrounding paddock areas. She didn't know Jesse very well. Clay had just hired her as a trainer and ranch hand at the Flying E. Sophie couldn't see for the tears running down her face, but she got out of the car and ran toward Jesse with sheer desperation urging her on.

"Sophie? What is it? What's wrong?"

"Your truck. May I please borrow your truck?"

"Sure." Frowning, Jesse pushed her hand down deep inside her jeans pocket and pulled out a key fob with several keys. Selecting one, she handed it to Sophie and pointed. "It's the green Dodge over there. Is there anything I can do?"

"No. This is good enough. I'll arrange to have it back to you as fast as I possibly can." With that she ran for the green pickup. What a total and complete fool she had been.

As she pulled out of the parking lot, she saw Clay running around the corner of the building toward her and she floored it, almost spinning out of control. The last thing she needed or wanted were a bunch of excuses from Clay. *I didn't know she would be here. It didn't mean anything.* The hell it didn't. It meant everything. This wasn't some surprise birthday party full of strippers and gags. It was real. And the sooner she got away from here, the better.

How she made it to the small cottage, she would never know. It was pure luck that she didn't rear-end someone or get broadsided. If there were red lights, she never saw them. Stop signs didn't exist. All she had was one single thought: How could he do this to her? Over the years she'd thought a lot of things both good and bad about him. His past had made him hard, moody and arrogant, but never cruel. At least never to her. Their time together flashed through her mind. The bond they'd formed when he'd struggled to overcome his injuries. The camaraderie in the new office. Watching the new foals. Long horseback rides in the wild country where she always felt safe with Clay near her. More recently, the romantic interludes where she had melted into his strong, powerful arms. The feeling he'd given her that she was the only woman in the world for him. The realization that they had created a new life. Had it all been a ruse? Had it all been a dream? Surely he wouldn't have gone to the trouble just to take her to his bed, especially when he could have practically any woman he wanted and with a lot less effort.

Once she'd arrived at the cottage, she lost no time throwing things into a suitcase. What she didn't take with her today she could always send for.

She grabbed her cell and punched the number for her landlord, Whit Daltry.

"Whit? This is Sophie."

"Hey there. How's it going?"

"Actually, not so good." It took a few minutes to explain about her father's illness, having to stop periodically and restrain her emotions.

"I've got to go home. I can arrange for you to receive the remaining rent. I think there are about four months left on the lease."

"Forget it, Sophie. Don't give it another thought. You do what you have to do. Family comes first."

His words brought the tears to her eyes once again. He really was such a nice man. It was too bad Clay couldn't be more like him.

"Good luck to you, Sophie. Look, I'm going to hold the cottage for a couple of months in case things work out and you want to come back."

"I won't be coming back, Whit. But thanks for the offer."

"Not my business, but does Clay know?"

"Yeah. I just told him."

And he told me. Loud and clear.

* * *

The look on Sophie's face when she'd stepped into his office was something that would haunt Clay for the rest of his life. He pushed Carla Maxwell off his lap and stood up, not really caring if she made it to her feet or fell on the floor. She actually had the audacity to look shocked that he had pushed out of her arms.

He was furious. If anything had ever been a setup, this was it. It was too perfectly timed to be anything else.

"What in the hell are you doing here?"

"Excuse me? I don't know what you mean," she said in an angry tone as she straightened her dress.

"You know exactly what I mean. My only question is who put you up to it."

"Nobody put me up to anything! I received your email and I thought… You made it clear you wanted us to get back together," she snapped. "I assume you've changed your mind."

"I never sent you any email."

When Clay continued to glare, she walked to a chair next to the office door and pulled her cell phone out of her purse. After searching for a few seconds, she held out the phone to Clay.

True to her word, there was an email to Carla sent from his account. Only Clay didn't know anything about this. Months ago Clay would have taken the temptation but the thought of Sophie carrying his child had awakened feelings of protectiveness and possessiveness. He wanted nothing to do with another woman.

But how was this possible? The answer came to him immediately. Someone had hacked into his system. He couldn't help but speculate what else they'd done. And could this somehow be related to the attack on Everest?

His cell phone began to ring. When he gazed at the display, he saw it was Whit Daltry.

"Yeah," he answered, turning away from a still-sulking Carla. "How's it going?"

"Clay, this isn't any of my business, but are you aware Sophie has left?"

"I know she left here."

"She's gone. She called me to arrange to pay out the last months of her lease. Of course, I told her not to worry about it. She was packed and on her way to the airport."

"What?"

"She said she'd told you. I decided to call and butt in just in case she hadn't, seeing how close the two of you are. Is there anything I can do?"

"No, but thanks anyway. Oh, and, Whit? Someone hacked my phone. I think they might have Sophie's, too."

"Are you thinking what I'm thinking?"

"That it's the same SOB who has systemically

targeted people here in Royal? Yeah, it has Maverick's fingerprints all over it."

"I'll call a meeting for tomorrow at the TCC. We need to know if anything has gone on with anybody else and share your latest info."

"I'll try and make it. Just send me the time."

"Will do."

When the call ended, Clay again turned to face Carla.

"My apologies to you," he said, his hands on his hips. "Apparently someone hacked my phone and thought they would have some fun at our expense. I didn't send that email to you."

"Well, isn't this just my luck." She walked toward the door, giving Clay a wink as she passed. "If you ever change your mind, you know how to reach me."

Clay ran his fingers through his dark hair. Sophie was gone. He should go after her. Every cell in his body was on high alert to do just that. But he could talk himself blue in the face and he wouldn't be able to convince her to come back. Maybe he would have had a chance—if he hadn't screwed it up when she'd first told him about the baby. But her two simple words, *I'm pregnant*, had struck him dumb. He had always been so careful. Even back in the day when he'd landed in bed with a hot lady, drunk on his ass after a rodeo celebration in some bar, he'd always remembered to use protection. It had become as automatic as breathing.

Clay couldn't specifically remember if he'd used condoms that first night he'd taken Sophie to his bed. But then, actually getting to make love to the prim and proper Ms. Sophie had had him in so many knots, and he hadn't been able to get enough of her. Usually he was good for one, maybe two times in a night. With Sophie, his hunger had been insatiable and he'd taken her over and over and over. Apparently, at least one of those times he'd failed to grab a condom, which resulted in the pregnancy.

Clearly he had made a mistake. Now the question was, what to do about it? Maybe Whit was wrong. Maybe she hadn't left as yet. In a dead run, he jumped into his pickup truck and spun gravel as he headed to the cottage. He didn't have a clue what to say. He would have to wing it. Groveling would definitely be on the list. Just let him be in time to catch her before she disappeared from his life forever.

Sophie was in the process of placing suitcases into Jesse May's pickup when Clay rounded the corner and pulled up behind her. Her face, she knew, was still red from the tears she'd shed over Clay. But it was his problem. Someday he would regret it but that was on him to discover.

"Sophie," Clay said as he approached her. "Where are you going?"

She refused to look at him. Why waste her breath answering stupid questions?

"Just please go away and leave me alone. You've done quite enough."

"Sophie, I did not want that woman in my office. She is ancient history. Carla received an email from my account asking her to come to my office. I didn't send it. I wouldn't know how to contact her, so I couldn't have sent it. And if I was going to see her again, it wouldn't be in the office."

"Your office is in your house. Very convenient."

Sophie finished stowing her luggage and walked to the driver's side door.

"So that's it? You're going to believe some woman I haven't seen in ten years over me." It sounded like a statement rather than a question.

"It wasn't what I heard—it was what I saw." She turned to face him. "Explain how a woman you didn't invite to your office and didn't want to see again managed to straddle your lap and kiss you all over your face. How did that transpire, Cole?"

"She caught me off guard..."

"Off guard. Clay, you're wearing that excuse out. I don't know why you insist on using it. You need to come up with something new."

"What I can say? I don't know what you expect from me anymore. You keep catching me off guard, too. I had no idea you were going to tell me you were pregnant. You kept me in the dark for weeks. How did you feel when you first suspected it? Were you shocked? Were you initially frightened? Were you concerned about what would happen next? What was your reaction when your mother first called about your father's heart condition? You can't have prepared for such a thing. I definitely wasn't prepared for any of this. Yet you think the worst of me. It isn't fair. And you expect me to behave a certain way without giving me the chance to figure out what's going on with you."

"I don't expect anything from you, Clay. I've already told you that. But you could have waited until I left before you started dating again. Especially in consideration of the fact I'm carrying your child. I really don't think that is too much to ask."

Even if nothing had happened with that blonde, Clay was not the type to settle down. She needed to return to Indiana—her parents needed her at home—and she would have the baby there.

When he started to object again, she interrupted him. "I'll let you know when the baby is born. It should be sometime in January. And don't worry, you can have all the visitation you want." Her voice broke on the last words, as she struggled not to show weakness.

She had to leave. She had to get into the truck and head to the airport. She had to get as far away from Clay Everett as she possibly could. She was barely holding it together. Her anger gave her what strength she had. At the very least she had thought Clay was her friend. But friends wouldn't do what he'd done and come forward with a basket full of excuses instead of apologies. But then again, how sincere would his apologies have been?

This had gone so wrong. All of it. Everything. Clay's bull-riding accident had been the beginning. It set into motion things that should have never happened. He should never have taken up permanent residence at his ranch. His office should have never moved there. Everest wouldn't exist and the easygoing cowboy would never have shucked his jeans, cowboy hat and boots for a suit and tie. And she never would have moved to Royal, Texas.

The what-ifs spun around in her head like a whirlwind on the dry desert floor. What if she'd never let herself be seduced by Clay? What if she'd just left when she found out she was pregnant and moved back home without a word? What if she were a different type of person whose strength and resilience to say no would have superseded a yes when he made his intentions known at the masked ball in May? What if she didn't love him? Would it make this easier?

"Sophie, don't do this. Don't leave."

There was nothing else to say. She pulled her door closed, put the key in the ignition and started the engine. As she drove away, all she could see through blurry eyes was Clay in the rearview mirror.

Thirteen

Clay watched as Sophie drove down the street, around a corner and out of sight. He couldn't believe she was gone. How had he screwed this up so badly?

Returning to the ranch, he couldn't help but notice that Sophie's car was still there, which struck him as odd. In the house he automatically turned toward the office. Her space was cleared and neat as a pin. Gone were her weekly *People* magazines and the romance books she always kept on the credenza behind her desk. In fact, all that remained of her presence was the screen saver on the two computer monitors: a running horse, its mane and tail blowing in the wind. In the background were the magnificent Guadalupe Mountains.

Sophie loved this part of the world. She loved the haunting beauty of the desert as much as the towering mountain peaks with the thick groves of pine. She took great joy in the animals, from the tortoise to the antelope, although she didn't suffer any love lost for the mountain lion. He smiled at the memory of their shared night in the cabin near the branding site.

And she seemed to really like working with him. Especially in the years since the accident, she had not just been his assistant, she'd been his friend and his supporter. She was smart and knew her job and his, as well; she was independent enough that if pushed, she could do both. She was going to be missed in the office and out. Especially out.

She was the most amazingly beautiful woman he'd ever met yet unlike most, she didn't wear a ton of makeup or tight-fitting clothes to show off her figure and impress him. She left it to her smile and her dancing blue eyes and hands so soft it was like being touched by a warm silk mitten. And when she succumbed to his touch and his kisses, she went from a kitten to a cougar in the blink of an eye. She never played coy, never minced her words, sometimes to her detriment, especially in the office if his mood was bad enough. But 99 percent of the time, she was right and thankfully, he'd had enough good sense to realize that before he said or did something he would later regret. Until now.

Probably before the accident, definitely after, he was flawed as hell. He knew he was a hardheaded, arrogant son of a bitch and Iron Heart had provided scars and a permanent limp to go along with his flawed insides. Yet Sophie made him feel so alive, as though he could accomplish anything. Granted, he was a risk taker by nature, but she smoothed out the bumps and made him think twice before jumping into the fire. Consequently, he'd accomplished a lot more than he probably could have without her.

Sophie Prescott was going to be missed in every way from A to Z. And he was going to regret his part in her leaving for a very long time. He'd made a lot of mistakes in his life and he would probably make many more. But the worst of them were with Sophie.

If there was one single thing about this fiasco that was in the remotest sense positive, it was that he'd realized he was totally and completely in love with Sophie Prescott. He would not—could not—live his life without her in it.

He was the kind of man who went after what he wanted and that was not going to change. Not chasing after Sophie was one mistake he would not make. And if he could convince her to come back, it wouldn't be enough just to have her in his bed anymore. He wanted more; he needed more. He wanted to make a life with her and their baby. He just hoped she would be willing to listen to him. *He would make her listen.* He intended to convince Sophie to come back with him and dammit, he would not take no for an answer.

The flight to Indiana was long. Sophie had a lot of time to reflect on what had gone down. Clay was probably telling her the truth about Carla but that was only one incident with one woman and there were hundreds who would happily take her place. On his lap, in his arms and in his bed. The dark, brooding, impossibly handsome man who now carried the scars of battles won and lost in the arena was a temptation to women everywhere. The full lips, with dimples on both sides and those deep grooves that showed off that slow smile, would have most women feeling the heat from the beginning. If Sophie closed her eyes, she could see the passion lighting his emerald-green gaze, could hear his voice as he made demands and whispered encouragement that sent them both to the moon. His big hands, callused and strong, could bring out all kinds of intimate feelings. Dressed in a dark suit and tie, with his demeanor and no-nonsense attitude, he took command over a boardroom. Clay Everett was the most amazing man she'd ever met or would ever meet. She felt a slight blush run up her neck and over her face for ever thinking she would be the one he wanted. What a foolish idea. But at least she had one thing no other woman had: Clay's baby growing inside of her. An unknown and unintended gift she would cherish the rest of her life.

Although her mother had sounded shocked that Sophie had left her employment with Clay permanently, she was nonetheless delighted to know Sophie was on her way home. Her father had made it through the surgery without any complications and was doing great; at this rate, he'd be able to return home in a week. Her older sister was there with him while their mom picked Sophie up at the international airport in nearby Indianapolis. The thought of seeing her family again after so many years was exciting but still couldn't override the sadness of leaving Clay.

When and how had her time at Everest become so entangled and perplexing? Probably about the time she fell in love with its owner and CEO. She'd fought the feeling when it hit, tried to ignore it when it refused to go away and finally gave in to the sheer pleasure of being in love. Whether he'd ever felt anything for her or merely saw her as a new conquest, she couldn't honestly say. She only knew Clay had always made her feel special. Whether that was his standard mode of operation with most women, she didn't know. But it was enough to propel her into his arms all the while trying to deny that it was exactly where she wanted to be. Forever.

She should have seen the mistake coming. She should've known a life in love with Clay Everett was not a lasting thing. He wasn't a man who would ever settle down with one woman and want a family and children. It was only since his accident that he'd spent more than a month in the same place. It was a life much too tame for him to be content. His mind-set was more in tune with taking on a wild Brahma bull.

He'd never told her he loved her. Even when she had blurted it out during their lovemaking, he hadn't said anything in return. Her heart had withered a little at the time. Now the sorrow had spread throughout her body. She wanted to curl up and die. She had never seen herself as one of those girls who silently grieved while she watched the man she loved go on to other relationships. But that was pretty much what she'd done. Caught in her own inability to conceal her love, she had, by her admission, put their relationship in a very precarious setting. Had he grimaced when she told him she loved him? Surely she wasn't the first.

And she wouldn't be the last.

Sophie and her mother's first stop was the hospital. Visiting with her father did wonderful things for Sophie's self-esteem; he was just so excited to see her. And he looked great, considering what he'd just gone through. But even seeing that he was going to be okay hadn't taken away all the pain she carried inside. She left with a promise to come visit him again tomorrow.

"You remember where your old room is," her mom said as she and her sister carried her luggage inside the small white frame house. "I put fresh linens on the bed, gave the room a good cleaning and opened the windows to let in some fresh air. Both your and Susan's rooms have been closed for a while."

"I'm so glad you're here." Susan's arms came around her. "I've got to get back to work in Indianapolis next week, but that will give us a few days together. Did Mom tell you the amazing news?"

Sophie frowned. "No." She looked across the room at her mother. "She didn't say anything about anything, really."

"I wasn't going to overwhelm you your first second home, but…" Sophie noticed the tears welling in her mom's eyes. "I've been awarded my PhD. All those years of studying and research finally paid off."

"Oh, Susan!" Sophie hugged her sister. "That's so awesome! Congratulations!"

"That's not all… I'm engaged." She held out her left hand. On the fourth finger was an amazing engagement ring. While delighted for her sister, Sophie couldn't help the tears that stung her eyes. "That's wonderful news!" Sophie proceeded to put on an act like none other.

"We're getting married next summer then flying to the Bahamas for the honeymoon. Grady said we will have to live in Indianapolis, but we'll be less than an hour away from Mom and Dad. I'm hoping to get on the faculty at Purdue with Grady."

"Isn't that great?" their mother interrupted.

"It sure is," Sophie agreed and smiled. If only Clay could be here to share the joy.

"So." Susan looked at Sophie. "I hear you're going to be a mother! That's wild, Sophie. It's good news, but strange to think of my kid sister having a baby." She laughed and gave Sophie another hug. "Are you going to have it here or back in Texas?"

"Here." She swallowed hard to keep the disappointment from showing. She would give anything to have her son or daughter in Royal, Texas, to raise the baby near its father. But it wasn't feasible. Clay, if he cared, would have to come here. "After it's born, I'll find a job and rent a little house. Maybe I can do some substitute teaching between now and then."

She hadn't really thought this through but it made sense. She had enough in her savings to buy a used car and carry her for several months. If she could find a job in spite of what she'd done back when she was a senior in high school, it would work out okay. She was serious when she'd told Clay she wanted nothing from him. She wasn't about to leave him one day and call him asking for money the next. She'd definitely want child support, but wouldn't ask for a dime before then.

"Are you hungry?" her mom asked.

"I would love a bowl of cereal, if you have some."

"Cereal? Is that all you want to eat?"

"Come on, Soph, I'll help you find it," Susan said. "I want to hear more about Royal, Texas. Did you really work for a billionaire? I'll bet he was a hunk."

The next few days slowly crept by. It was good being in her childhood home with her family. Her father did so well in recovery that he was released early from the hospital, and caring for him took Sophie's mind off her troubles a little bit.

She realized she should've made the trip home a long time ago, for Christmas or another holiday. At first she'd avoided coming back to Tipton County because of what happened her senior year in high school. After that, she'd immersed herself in her new job, wanting to do the best for Cole that she could, especially after the accident. One month led to the next and the next until the years had passed.

While she tried to keep the smile on her face whenever someone was nearby, she knew her parents sensed her sadness. Thankfully, neither one said a word. But her mom knew. About Clay and the baby.

About leaving him. About the turmoil and pain that was ripping through Sophie's heart.

She had been on pins and needles every time her parents' phone rang. And she faithfully kept her cell charged. But no call came through. By the fifth day, she was forced to accept the finality of the situation. Clay would never call. Maybe he'd finally had his security division run a check on her background and had found out her history. That, combined with the ball and chain she offered, was more than enough to keep him at a distance. At least until February, when the baby was due to be born. She believed he truly cared about the baby. It was just the kind of man he was. He would be a good father. Of that she had no doubt. But it would be fatherly time spent with his son or daughter when she wasn't around. Tea parties in the grand salon if a girl. Riding his first horse and learning to rope if a boy.

Then one day, as she was heading outside to do some gardening, the tears sprang to her eyes before she reached the back door. This time there was no holding back. Dropping down onto the outside stoop, she gave in to the misery she'd kept inside for so long, until the sobs overwhelmed her and she could no longer feel or think of Clay Everett.

Fourteen

The rumbling sound of thunder filled the far-off horizon. Sophie looked up to see an almost cloudless blue sky. Odd, she thought. But then out here in the miles and miles of flat terrain of the farming communities, sound had a way of traveling great distances.

She was sitting outside the house under the shade of the large tree on the bench swing her father had built when she was only a child. She had so many memories, most of them good, of growing up in this small, rural American town with a population under a thousand. For eighteen years it had been her world. Then tragedy had struck and she'd spirited off to a college in a distant county. Ironically, her world had expanded. From there she'd taken a job working for a Texas rancher and part-time rodeo cowboy. Now she was back where she started. She'd come full circle. And she'd brought with her new memories, experiences she would always cherish, and soon a child who would grow up between two completely different worlds: the quiet farming community Sophie had always called home and the Texas ranch of the baby's billionaire father.

The sound of the thunder grew increasingly louder until Sophie realized it wasn't thunder but an aircraft of some sort. Whatever it was, it was big and headed in this direction. The numbing thought ran through her mind that it might be Clay. Would he come here? No. That was a ridiculous idea. They had said everything there was to say before she left. He had his corporation to run, Maverick to fend off and an entire ranching operation to manage. Although Clay had help with most of it, the responsibility still rested on his shoulders. He wouldn't have time to come all the way to Indiana because of her. Even if the time was there, there was no reason.

She had to stop this. She had to let go of that last lingering strand of hope. It was over. Whatever they had at one time, imagined or real, was over. She needed to focus on the future. She needed to apply for a substitute-teaching position for the upcoming fall start to the school year. She had to find reliable transportation. She had to find a doctor, an ob-gyn. She really should find her own place to live but until the baby was born she might be of help to her parents if she just stayed here. Although it was a bit cramped, they had made the room.

The sound grew louder. Then, as though dropping out of the heavens, a helicopter appeared some few miles away. As it came closer, she could just make out the lettering on the side: *EVERETT.* It was Clay or someone from his company. Her heart rate sped up and she swallowed several times, her eyes glued to the aircraft.

The sheets and towels her mom had hung out on the line to dry in the fresh air began to move as though they were desperate to escape the storm that was headed their way. The trees swayed, the grasses parted as the helicopter lowered out of the sky.

Sophie didn't know whether to stand there or run into the house. The turbulence caused dirt particles to swirl around her face, getting into her eyes and nose. With no landing pad available, the pilot had no choice but to land on the loosely packed earth of the plowed field directly behind the house. Giving the helicopter one last glance, she bolted toward the house. She didn't need to stand there fighting the turbulence and she didn't want to appear overanxious for Clay to step out of the helicopter. She didn't want him here. She was making some headway in coming to peace with their parting and she didn't want to face his questions and excuses. Still, part of her wanted to know what had brought him here.

The blades of the helicopter slashed the air as the chopper set down. With one backward glance, Sophie slipped into the back door of her parents' house and closed it behind her. She realized she was trembling. She wanted so badly to see Clay again but when he left, the pain would be fresh and new. The thought of his wonderful scent, those green eyes and easy smile, the warmth and gentleness of his strong hands, made her breathing become shallow. It would take her months to get over that yearning, if not years. She tried to be strong. But her ability to resist him was weak.

Her mother was in the kitchen, cleaning up after their supper. When Sophie had asked to help she was told no, to just relax, watch TV or maybe go outside and enjoy the remains of the day. Now her mom's eyes were glued to the small window over the kitchen sink, as she no doubt watched the helicopter land.

"Is that Clay?" she apparently couldn't refrain from asking.

"That would be my guess," Sophie replied. How many people did they know who would fly in and land the helicopter in the backyard like that?

"Aren't you going out to welcome him?"

Sophie couldn't hold back a snort. "If he wants to talk to me, he obviously knows where I live."

Casually, Sophie walked into the empty living room. "Where are Susan and Dad?" It was amazing how calm she could sound when her heart was beating out of her chest.

"Your father is upstairs taking a nap and Susan went over to Mildred Sullivan's to pick up a pie she baked to welcome you home. Apple. It's your favorite."

"Oh."

Where was Clay? Sophie's hands formed tight fists at her sides to try to prevent herself from going to a window and peering outside. Just then the front doorbell rang.

Her feet wouldn't move. She wanted to run to the door, throw it open and fall into his arms. But those arms and strong embrace were not hers any longer, if they ever had been. She had no right to expect anything other than a cordial hello followed by mute discomfort and awkwardness.

The bell rang again.

"Sophie." Her mother stood on the threshold between the kitchen and den. "Answer the door."

She did as she was asked, and there stood Clay on the porch. He was so tall and big, it seemed impossible that those wide shoulders would make it through the door. He stole her breath. Her eyes bounced from his face to his chest, not wanting to meet his eyes for fear of what she would find there. Pity? Probably. Arrogance? Always. Concern? Probably not.

"Sophie? Are you going to invite me in?"

She pushed open the outside screen door and Clay stepped into the room. Unbidden, her eyes went to his handsome face. There was no pity. No arrogance. There was concern and something else she couldn't quite make out. He looked like hell. His eyes were red-rimmed and he had a grayish pallor to his face.

"So, how have you been?"

"Good. Fine. Clay, what are you doing here?"

"Hello, Clay," her mother called from the kitchen. "How are you?"

"Good, Mrs. Prescott, thanks."

"Would you like to sit down?" Sophie asked. With the initial shock over, she was finally remembering her manners.

"Actually, is there someplace we can go and talk in private? Outside maybe?"

Sophie didn't want to be alone with him. But she understood Clay well enough to know he would not leave until he said or did what he'd come all this way to.

"Sure, we can go outside," she agreed. "I was out there enjoying a beautiful day until someone plopped a helicopter in my backyard, blowing dust up my nose and into my eyes."

"Sorry about that," he said as he opened the front door, indicating she should proceed.

The small country lane bordered by shade trees at the end of the meandering driveway seemed as good a place as any to talk. Clay shortened his stride to match hers as they made their way along the cool, shadowy path.

"I screwed up, Sophie. I want you to come back."

"No."

"Look, I know I reacted wrong when you told me about the baby. I was still riding the high from being in your arms, from making love to you, when you told me. It took a few seconds for what you said to really soak in. Then, I don't know, I didn't know what to say. I can honestly say that was a totally new experience for me."

"Okay. I get that."

"And the Carla thing? Somebody hacked my email account. If you received a text or email asking you to come into my office, they hacked yours, too, because I didn't send it. Carla got a message, supposedly from me, asking her to come by my office because I wanted to get back together with her. Which was funny because we never were an item to begin with. I did not send that email."

"Okay."

"Okay? What does that mean exactly?"

"It means that I believe you. It also means that I will absolutely not ruin your life by tying you down to a wife and family. I respect you too much to do that."

Suddenly he seized her arm and spun her around. Before she could utter a protest, his lips covered hers in a deep kiss that singed all her senses. His tongue entered the cavern of her mouth, filling her, demanding a response. His lips, his taste, were so familiar. The scent of his aftershave… Then he was pulling back, but not far.

"I'm in love with you, Sophie Prescott. I want to marry you. Not because you're pregnant. Not because I feel a responsibility, although both of those things are true. I want you in my life now and forever. I intended to come here the day you arrived and thought, no—give her a chance to calm down. I knew you were angry and I guess you had a good reason to be. Anyway, I made myself stay away until now. But it almost killed me. I need you in my bed, in my arms and in my life. And I always will."

The tears welled in her eyes at the sincerity in Clay's voice. Silently she shook her head. It would be a mistake to accept him, but she'd made plenty of mistakes. What was one more? But he had to know who she was. He had to know she was a criminal. She had to tell Clay about her past, about what she'd done. About how that elderly man had lost his life partly because of her actions. It didn't matter if he was intoxicated and shouldn't have been there, as some people had claimed. No one in her group should have been there, either. The bottom line was he *had* been there and no one had noticed him. And he had died.

Clay was a hard man, as tough as they came. He'd seen a lot in his life. But he'd never taken another person's life. She turned away from him.

"Sophie, please don't do this."

"You don't know what you're saying, Clay. You don't know the kind of person you're talking to. I'm not the innocent you think I am. When Everest was facing all those false rumors, you ran a check on all the employees who've been with you the past two years. You should have gone back five years."

"What?" He placed his hand on her shoulder and turned her to face him. "What are you talking about?"

"Me. I'm talking about me. If you had gone back five years, you would've found my record. Well, maybe not, because I was seventeen and juvenile records are generally sealed." She looked up into the handsome face now frowning at what she was saying. "I killed a man, Clay. Me and four friends went into an empty barn to experiment with smoking a cigarette. We screwed up, dropped a match and caught the barn on fire. We thought the barn was abandoned. But there was an elderly man asleep on the hay in the back corner. He died." She shook her head. "Some mother your kid is going to have, huh?"

Clay stood before her shaking his head and she steeled herself for his rejection.

"I caught you off guard again, didn't I?"

"Sophie, that sounds like something any teen could have done. You were young. It was an accident. You and your friends didn't know the man was there."

"Not an excuse."

"Did you receive any probation?"

"We had to get jobs after school and pay for the owner's barn. And we get to spend a lifetime remembering what we did. You don't want someone like me in your life. It fills me with horror at the thought the baby might someday find out."

"Everyone is entitled to make mistakes, Sophie. Granted, burning down a barn might be a little extreme, but by far it's not the worst mistake that's ever been made. You didn't know the man was passed out in the barn. How could you when he was covered with hay?"

She blinked. More than once. "How did you know about the hay?"

"Your mom. She called. We talked. She was afraid I had found out about this situation and rejected you because of it. She wanted to make sure I had all the facts. I assured her that was absolutely not the case. I'm in love with you, Sophie. I hope you will believe that. You could never do anything to drive me away."

Then Clay dropped to one knee in front of her, his

big hands holding hers. "Marry me, Sophie Prescott. If you love me after all I've put you through then marry me. Don't make me go another day without you."

The joy she felt could match none other on earth as she bounded into his arms, knocking them both to the ground. Laughing, Clay kissed her lovingly and deeply before helping Sophie to her feet and showing concern that she was okay.

Her mother and dad and Susan were waiting just inside the door when the couple walked back to the farmhouse and up the steps.

"I take it congratulations are in order." Her dad beamed and shook Clay's hand. "Welcome to the family. And thank you, Clay."

"Dad, what are you thanking him for?" Sophie laughed. "Surely I'm not that hard to give away."

"No," her father replied, moisture forming in his own eyes. "I'll let Clay tell you. It's his place to do so. But let me just say it's thanks to him I can look forward to walking my youngest daughter down the aisle."

Clay shrugged. "I just contacted a couple of specialists I know. They arranged the transfer. Luck did the rest."

It didn't take Sophie half a second to realize she owed her father's life to Clay. He had taken the time and gone to the effort to arrange everything. Her dad's new heart was thanks to him. Tears misted her eyes as the reality hit home.

"If you're ready," Clay said to Sophie, "we need to be headed out. There are some vital things I need to address on the flight home."

After hugs and congratulations all around, Sophie excused herself and entered the bedroom she'd been sharing with her sister. Pulling a small suitcase down from a high shelf in the closet, she set about packing the few things she would need until she could go shopping. Her mother joined her with Susan right behind. Together the three of them, with hugs and laughter, filled more than one suitcase.

Clay scooped up the bags and after saying goodbye to her family, he walked toward the chopper, Sophie at his side. Clay helped her inside and got in behind the controls. He circled the small house once before taking off toward Indianapolis International Airport.

"So," she said, her hand in his, the brilliant four-carat engagement ring glistening in the evening sunlight. "What's so important that you just have to get to Indianapolis?"

"The 747 is waiting there. No way can I wait to get you home before I make love to you again. If I recall, you may have changed your mind about flying."

Sophie grinned.

"I feel the need to reinforce that newly found love," he said, squeezing her hand. "All the way to Texas."

Epilogue

The wedding took place a week later with an impatient Clay still suggesting they elope to Vegas. But Sophie wanted the memory of her wedding day with her family and friends around her. And she insisted on being married in Royal, Texas.

While Clay wanted to give her the moon—anything she wanted for their special day, as well as the rest of their lives—in the end she kept it simple. A country wedding on the ranch in a small chapel that had been constructed on a rise looking out over the land they both loved so much. Clay looked extraordinarily handsome in his tux—complete with Western boots and Stetson—as he dismounted the black stallion and waited for his bride to walk down the aisle on her dad's arm.

Arriving in Clay's grandmother's carriage, laced with ribbons of blue and gold and pulled by two white horses, Sophie couldn't take her eyes off the man of her dreams, her cowboy love forever and always.

It was a day of love and laughter and best wishes for the future.

And many more flights on Clay's 747.

As she walked toward her future husband, she smiled at the memory.

"Where are we going next?" Clay whispered, his green eyes twinkling as though he knew exactly what she was thinking. And he did.

"Does it matter?" she asked and grinned.

Solemnly he slowly shook his head, his eyes holding hers.

It didn't matter at all.

* * * * *

August 2017: TEMPTED BY THE WRONG TWIN by USA TODAY *bestselling author Rachel Bailey*

September 2017: TAKING HOME THE TYCOON by USA TODAY *bestselling author Catherine Mann*

October 2017: BILLIONAIRE'S BABY BIND by USA TODAY *bestselling author Katherine Garbera*

November 2017: THE TEXAN *TAKES A WIFE by* USA TODAY *bestselling author Charlene Sands*

December 2017: BEST MAN UNDER THE MISTLETOE by Jules Bennett

***

If you're on Twitter, tell us what you think of Harlequin Desire! #harlequindesire

Read on for a sneak peek of
DOWN HOME COWBOY
by New York Times *bestselling author Maisey Yates.*
When rancher and single dad Cain Donnelly
moves to Copper Ridge, Oregon, to make
a fresh start with his teenage daughter,
the last thing he wants is to risk his heart again.
So why can't he keep his eyes—or his hands—
off Alison Davis, the one woman in town
guaranteed to complicate his life?

"Hey, Bo," Cain called, looking around the kitchen and living room area for his daughter, who was on the verge of being late for her second week on the job. "Are you ready to go?"

He heard footsteps hit the bottom landing, followed by a disgusted noise. "Do you have to call me that?"

"Yes," he said, keeping his tone serious. "Though I could always go back to the full name. Violet Beauregarde the Walking Blueberry." She'd thought that nod to *Charlie and the Chocolate Factory* was great. Back when she was four and all he'd had to do was smile funny to get her to belly laugh.

"Pass."

"I have to call you at least one horrifying nickname a week. All the better if it slips out in public."

"Is there public in Copper Ridge? Because I've yet to see it."

"Hey, you serve the public as part of your job at the bakery."

"The presence of humanity does not mean the presence of culture."

"Chill out, Sylvia Plath. Your commitment to being angry at the world is getting old." He shook his head, looking at his dark-haired, green-eyed daughter, who was now edging closer to being a woman than being that round, rosy-cheeked little girl he still saw in his mind's eye.

"Well, you don't have to bear witness to it today. Lane is giving me a ride into town."

Cain frowned. He still hadn't been in to see Violet at work. In part because she clearly didn't want him to. But he had assumed that once she was established and feeling independent she wouldn't mind if he took her to Pie in the Sky.

Apparently, she did.

"Great," he said. "I have more work to do around here anyway."

"The life of a dairy farmer is never dull. Well, no, it's always dull. It just never stops." Violet walked over to the couch where she had deposited her purse yesterday and picked it up. "Same with baking pies, I guess."

"Are you ready to go, Violet?" Lane came breezing into the room looking slightly disheveled, Cain's younger brother Finn closely behind her, also looking suspiciously mussed.

Absolutely no points for guessing what they had just been up to. Though he could see that Violet was oblivious. If she had guessed, she wouldn't be able to hide her reaction. Which warmed his heart in a way. That his teenage daughter was still pretty innocent about some things. That she was still young in some ways.

Hard to retain any sort of innocence when your mother abandoned you. And since he knew all about parental abandonment and how much it screwed with you, he was even angrier that his daughter was going through the same thing.

"Ready," Violet responded.

Even though it was a one-word answer, it lacked the edge usually involved in her responses to him. He supposed being jealous of his brother's girlfriend was a little bit ridiculous.

"Have fun," he said, just because he knew it would irritate her.

He had lost the power to make her laugh. To make her smile, with any kind of ease. So, he supposed he would just embrace his ability to irritate.

At least he excelled at that.

He could tell he had excelled yet again when she didn't smile at him as she left the room with Lane.

"Wait," Finn said, walking past him and grabbing Lane around the waist, turning her and kissing her deep.

It was all Cain could do to keep from groaning audibly. Between his horndog younger brothers and his incredibly happy other brother, he felt like sex was being thrown in his face constantly. Except not in a fun way that involved him having it.

Lane and Violet left, and Finn walked back into the living room. "I'm going to marry that woman," he said, the self-satisfied grin on his face scraping at Cain's current irritation.

"Have you asked her yet?"

"Not officially. But I'm going to. I want to spend the rest of my life with her."

"That's a long time. Trust me. Married years are different than regular years." He had way too much experience living with somebody who didn't even like him anymore. Way too much experience walking quietly through his own house so that he could avoid the conversation that needed to be had, or avoid the silence that seemed magnified when the two of them were in the same room.

He didn't think Finn would suffer the same fate, though. Finn and Lane had known each other for years, and they had been friends before they were a couple. Cain and Kathleen had been stupid and young. He had gotten her pregnant and wanted to do the right thing, instead of doing the kind of thing his father would do.

All in all, it wasn't the best foundation for a marriage.

For a while, they had tried. Both of them. He wasn't really sure when they had stopped.

"I hope you're right," Finn said, obnoxiously cheerful. "I hope every year with Lane feels like five. Because my time with her has been the best of my life."

Given the way they had grown up, Cain really didn't begrudge Finn his happiness. He was glad for his brother, in a way. When he wasn't busy feeling irritated by his own celibate status.

Though, in fairness to him, figuring out how to conduct a physical relationship while he was raising a teenage girl was pretty tricky. He had to set some kind of example. And casual sex wasn't exactly the one he was aiming for.

"Good for you," he said, sounding more annoyed than he had intended.

"How's the barn coming along?"

Cain was grateful for the change in subject. "It's coming."

"Show me."

His brother grabbed his hat off the shelf by the door, and Cain grabbed his own. Strange how this had become somewhat natural. How sharing a space with Finn, Alex and Liam—while annoying on occasion—was just starting to be life.

He took the steps on the front porch two at a time, inhaling the sharp, clear air. It was late summer, and in Texas about now walking outside would be like getting wrapped in a wet blanket. That was also on fire. He could honestly say he didn't miss that part of his adopted home state.

The Oregon coast ran a little cold for his taste, but he had to admit it was still nicer than sweltering. The wind whipped up, filtering through the pine trees and kicking up the smell of wood, hay and horse. If green had a smell, it would be that smell that rode the coastal air across the mountains. Fresh and heavy, all at the same time.

It was fastest to take a truck out to the old barn on the property, the one that had originally stood near the first house that had been built when their great-grandparents had bought the land. The house was long gone, but the barn still remained, and with all of his near-nonexistent free time, Cain had been fashioning the place into a house for Violet and himself.

After they parked, he and his brother walked through the still overgrown pathway that led up to the old barn.

"Wow," Finn said, stepping deeper into the room. "You've done a lot."

"New wiring," Cain said, gesturing broadly. "Insulation, Sheetrock. I need to work on interior walls. But, yeah, it's coming along. It will be fine for the two of us for the next couple of years. And when Violet leaves..."

Unbidden, an image of the beautiful redhead he had seen across the bar last night filtered into his mind's eye. Yeah, in a couple of years he would have a place to bring a woman like that.

Not that he couldn't go back to her place, or get a hotel, but he didn't want to have to explain his absence to a teenage girl who barely thought of him as human, much less wanted to realize he was actually just a guy with a sex drive and everything. Both of them would probably die from the humiliation of that.

"It'll be a pretty nice place," Finn said, and Cain was grateful his younger brother couldn't read his mind.

"Not bad. I know that I could pay somebody to finish it. But right now I'm kind of enjoying the therapy. I spent a long time managing things. Managing a big ranch, not actually working it. Managing my marriage instead of actually working at it. I'm ready to be hands-on again. This is the life that I'm choosing to build for myself. So I guess I better build it."

He knew that at thirty-eight his feelings of midlife angst were totally unearned, but having his wife leave had forced him into kind of a strange crisis point. One where he had started asking himself if that was it. If everything good that he was going to do was behind him.

So, he had left the ranch in Texas—the one he had spent so many years building up—walked away with a decent chunk of change, and packed his entire life up, packed his kid up, and gone to the West Coast to find… Something else to do. Something else to be. To find a way to reconnect with Violet.

So far, he'd found ranch work and little else. Violet still barely tolerated him in spite of everything he was doing to try to fix their lives, and he didn't feel any closer to moving forward than he had back in Texas.

He was just moved.

Finn's phone buzzed and he pulled it out of his pocket to check his texts. "Hey," he said, "can you pick up Violet tonight from work?"

"I thought Lane was doing it."

"It's her girls' night thing. She forgot."

Well, he had just been thinking that he needed to actually see where Violet worked. "Sure. Sounds good."

"What are you going to do until then?"

"I figured I would do some work in here."

Finn pushed his sleeves up, smiling. "Mind if I help?"

"Sure," Cain said. "Grab a hammer."

ALISON STARED AT the sunken cake sitting on the kitchen countertop and frowned. Then quickly erased the frown so that Violet wouldn't see it.

"I don't know what happened," Violet said, looking perturbed.

"You probably took it out too early. It's nothing a little extra icing can't fix. And it's my girls' night tonight, so I think it can be of use in that environment rather than being put up for sale."

Violet screwed up her face. "It's ugly."

"An ugly cake is still cake. As long as it doesn't have raisins it's fine."

"Oh, I didn't put any raisins in it."

Alison was slightly amused that her newest employee seemed to know about her raisin aversion, even if she didn't quite have cooking times down. Violet was a good employee, but she had absolutely no experience baking. For the most part, Alison had put her on the register, which she had picked up much faster than kitchen duties. But she tried to set aside a certain amount of time every shift to give Violet a chance to get some experience with the actual baking part of the bakery.

Maybe it wasn't as necessary to do with a teenager who had her first job as it was to do with some of the other women who came through the shop, desperately in need of work experience after years out of the workforce, but Alison was applying the same principles to Violet as she did to everyone else.

Right now she was short on staff, and even shorter on people who had the skill level she required with the baked goods to do any training. So while she could farm out Violet's register training, the cakes, pies and other pastries had to be done by her.

"I'll do better next time," Violet said, sounding

determined. Which encouraged Alison, because Violet hadn't sounded anything like determined when she had first come in looking for work. Violet was a sullen teenager of the first order. And even though she most definitely made an attempt to put on a good show for Alison, she was clearly in a full internal battle with her feelings on authority figures.

Having been a horrific teenager herself, Alison felt some level of sympathy for her. But also very little patience. Fortunately, Violet seemed to react well to her brand of no-nonsense response to attitude.

"You will do better next time," Alison said, "because I can eat one mistake cake, but if I have to continue eating them, my jeans aren't going to fit and then I'm going to have to buy new jeans, and that's going to have to come out of your paycheck."

She patted Violet on the shoulder then walked through the double doors that led from the kitchen and behind the counter. The shop was in its late-afternoon lull. A little too close to dinner for most people to be stopping in for pieces of pie.

A rush of air blew into the shop and Alison looked up just in time to see a tall, muscular man walk in through the blue door. A pang of recognition hit her in the chest before she even got a good look at him. She didn't need a good look at him. Because just like the first time she'd seen him, on the other side of Ace's bar, the feeling he created inside of her wasn't logical, wasn't cerebral. It was physical. It lived in her, and it superseded control.

For somebody who prized control, it was an affront on multiple levels.

He lifted his head and confirmed what her jittering nerves already knew. That beneath that dark cowboy hat was the face of the man who had most definitely been looking at her at the bar the night before.

He hadn't left town. He hadn't been a hallucinogenic expression of a fevered imagination. And he had found her.

The twist of attraction turned into something else, just for a moment. A strange kind of panic that she hadn't confronted for a long time. That somehow this man had found out who she was, had tracked her down.

No. That's not it. Even if he did, that doesn't make him crazy. It doesn't.

And more than likely he was just here for a piece of pie. She took a deep breath, steeling herself to look directly at him. Which was... Wow. He was hotter than she remembered. And that was saying something. She had first spotted him in the dim light of the bar, with a healthy amount of space between them.

Now, well, now the daylight was bright, and he was very close. And he was magnificent. The way that black T-shirt hugged all those muscles bordered on obscene, his dark green eyes like the deep of the forest beckoning her to draw close. Except, unlike the forest, his eyes didn't promise solitude and inner peace. No, it was something much more carnal. Or maybe that was just her aforementioned overheated imagination.

His jaw was covered by a neatly trimmed dark beard, and she would normally have said she wasn't a huge fan, but something about the beard on him was like flaunting an excess of testosterone. And she was in a very testosterone-starved state. So it was like stumbling onto water in a desert.

Of course, all of that hyperbole was simply that. His eyes weren't actually promising her anything; in fact, his expression was blank. And she realized that while he might look sexier to her today than he had that night, she might look unrecognizable to him.

Last night she had been wearing an outfit that at least hinted at the fact that she had a female figure. And she'd had makeup on. Plus, she'd gone to the effort to straighten her mass of auburn hair. Today, it was its glorious frizzy self, piled on top of her head, half captured in a rubber band, half pinned down with a pen. And as for makeup... Well, on days when she had to be at the bakery early, that was just not a happening thing.

Her apron disguised her figure, and beneath it, the button-up striped shirt that she had tucked into her jeans wasn't exactly vixen wear.

"Can I...? Can I help you?" She tucked a stray strand of hair behind her ear and found herself tilting her head to the side, her body apparently calling on all of the flirtation skills it hadn't used since she was eighteen years old.

Very immature, underdeveloped skills.

Suddenly, her lips felt dry, so she had to lick them. And when she did, heat flared in those forest green eyes that made her think maybe he did recognize her. Or, if he didn't, maybe his body did. Just like hers recognized his. *Oh, Lord.*

"Yes," he said, his voice much more…taciturn than she had imagined it might be. She hadn't realized until that moment that she had built something of a narrative around him. Brooding, certainly, because he had most definitely been brooding in the bar, but she had imagined he might flirt with a lazy drawl. Of course, it was difficult to tell with one word, but his voice had been clipped. Definitely clipped.

"I have a lot of different pie. I mean, a lot of different kinds. So, if you need suggestions…or a list… I can help."

"I'm not here for pie. I'm here to pick up my daughter…"

*Pick up DOWN HOME COWBOY,
the latest COPPER RIDGE novel
from Maisey Yates and HQN Books!*

COMING NEXT MONTH FROM

HARLEQUIN® *Desire*

Available August 8, 2017

HDCNM0717

Get 2 Free Books,

Plus 2 Free Gifts—

just for trying the Reader Service!

*When billionaire Linc Ballantyne's ex abandons not
one, but two children, he strikes up a wary deal with her
too-sexy sister. She'll be the nanny and they'll keep their
hands to themselves. But their temporary truce soon
becomes a temporary tryst!*

*Read on for a sneak peek at
THE CEO'S NANNY AFFAIR
by Joss Wood.*

Why Linc had ever agreed to meet with his ex-fiancée's
sister was confounding. But he'd heard something in her
voice, a note of panic and sorrow. Maybe something had
happened to Kari, and, if so, he needed to know what.
She was still his son's mother, after all.

Linc heard the light rap on the door and sucked in a
breath.

His first thought when he opened his front door to Tate
Harper was that he wanted her. Under him, on top of him,
up against the nearest wall…any way he could have her.

That thought was immediately followed by *Oh, crap,
not again.*

He knew the Harpers were trouble. Kari had been a
stunning woman, but her beauty, as he knew—and paid
for—had taken work. The woman standing behind the
stroller was effortlessly gorgeous. Her hair was a riot of

blond and brown, eyes the color of his favorite whiskey under arched eyebrows, and her skin, makeup-free, was flawless. This Harper sister's beauty was all natural and, dammit, so much more potent.

Linc, his hand on the doorknob, took a moment to draw in some much-needed air.

"Tate? Come on in."

She pushed the stroller into the hall with a white-knuckled grip. Linc, wincing at the realization that he was allowing a whole bunch of trouble to walk through his front door, was about to rescind his invitation. Then he made the mistake of looking into her eyes.

She'd jumped into the ring with Kari and had the crap kicked out of her, Linc realized. And, for some reason, she thought he could help her clean up the mess. And because his first instinct was to protect, to make things right, he wanted to wipe the fear from Tate's expression.

Linc closed his eyes and reminded himself to start using his brain.

He needed to hear Tate's story so he could hustle her out the door and get back to his predictable, safe, sensible world. She was pure temptation, and being attracted to his crazy ex's sister was a complication he most definitely did not need.

Don't miss
THE CEO'S NANNY AFFAIR
by Joss Wood, available August 2017 wherever
Harlequin® Desire books and ebooks are sold.

www.Harlequin.com

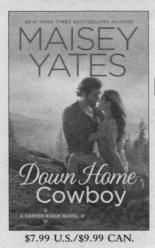